Smith's
MONTHLY

*Every Month Original
Novels, Stories, and Articles*

USA Today Bestselling Writer
Dean Wesley Smith

I0557598

TABLE OF CONTENTS

SHORT STORIES

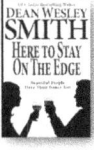

FULL NOVEL

SERIAL NOVEL

NONFICTION

SMITH'S MONTHLY ISSUE #33

All Contents copyright © 2016 Dean Wesley Smith
Published by WMG Publishing
Cover and interior design copyright © 2016 WMG Publishing
Cover art copyright © by Katya Triling/Dreamstime.com

The Writings and Opinions of
Dean Wesley Smith

Introduction
A NOVEL OUT OF THE BLUE

I seldom start a book or a story with an "idea" as most writers think of it. In fact, for me, starting a story with an idea is so rare, I can't remember the last time I did that. Until the novel *The Taft Ranch: A Thunder Mountain Novel* in this issue, that is.

So let me give you a few paths I take to writing a novel in general.

First, and the method I use the most. When I start a novel, I have written a short story and want to jump from the short story. I think the short story didn't finish the story the way it could be expanded.

When writing a novel like that, I honestly don't know where the story is going, but just that the story in the short story needs more than what I gave it.

A second way I start a novel (and most of my short stories) is that I get a title. I just type the title in and then start typing, wondering where my crazy mind is going to take me.

This is a lot like just picking up a book, opening to the first page, and starting to read without looking at the cover or the sales blurb.

Try that sometime. No cheating. Just grab a book at random, or have someone open up a book to the first page for you and start reading.

I love that experience of exploring and telling a story. I get to experience a story the same way the readers do. Wonderful fun for me.

A third way is from a piece of cover art.

Back in my traditional publishing days, I was hired a number of times to write a novel that would fit inside a cover the publisher already had. The best example of this is when I wrote a book for Jonathan Frakes called *Abductors*. I can tell you about it because he wanted my name on the inside title page. I wrote that book to the cover.

The fourth way I start a novel, and the one that seldom happens, is that I have an idea for a novel. Well, the novel in this issue started that way.

Thanks for the Support

Dean Wesley Smith

The idea was simple. I was in a conversation with my wife, Kristine Kathryn Rusch, when for some reason I heard myself say, "I wonder what would happen if someone got lost in time?"

And that was the idea. That simple.

With the Thunder Mountain series of books, getting lost in time is very, very difficult to do. And that made it a challenge.

And for a few days that was where it sat.

Then I saw this nifty piece of art that is on the cover and knew that would be the cover for the book. I came up with one of the main character's name, Lee Taft, who lived in the ranch on the cover, and off I went.

So the novel in this issue came from combining two of my ways of starting novels. I found a great cover and I came up with an "idea" which I almost never do.

I had a blast writing the novel. I hope you enjoy reading it as much as I did writing it.

—Dean Wesley Smith
Lincoln City, Oregon
June 11, 2016

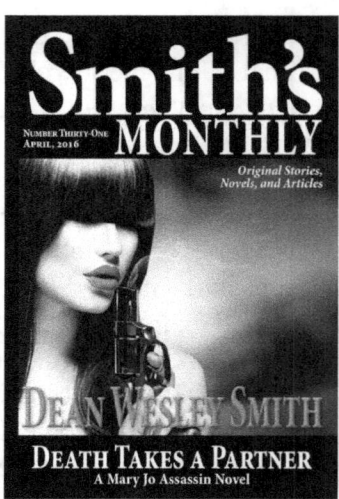

Coming Next Issue in *Smith's Monthly*
FREEZEOUT
A Cold Poker Gang Mystery

He calls himself The Presumptive.

Poker Boy thinks that might be the most stupid nickname he ever heard at a poker table.

So Poker Boy calls him Idiot Boy (but not to his face) because of the name and the guy's bad play.

But in Poker Boy's world, nothing ever turns out the way they look. Even for Idiot Boy.

THE RUDE IMPROBABLE PRESUMPTIVE
A Poker Boy Story

ONE

HE CALLED HIMSELF The Presumptive.

That might have been the most stupid nickname I have ever heard a guy call himself at a poker table.

But idiot boy (as I liked to call him, but not out loud) thought the name fit his poker playing, I guess making him the presumptive winner. Actually, from his poker game, his nickname should have been Long-Time Loser.

The game was a good one, a nice no-limit game at my home casino in the Oregon Mountains. Spirit Winds Casino was a small place in comparison to Vegas standards, yet friendly and welcoming.

I had jumped from my office in Las Vegas to the casino at 6 p.m. right after Patty had gone to work at the MGM Grand.

I had first checked on the progress of the luxury home we were having built in the mountains a few miles from the casino, and then managed to get into the no-limit game around 7 p.m. as it started up.

Patty didn't get off work until two in the morning, so I was looking forward to a fun night of poker and making a little money.

The Spirit Winds poker room was a great place with fifteen tables, a friendly staff, and brushes and dealers who knew how to keep the games fun and relaxed. As with everything in the casino, the wood and brown tones helped make the place feel relaxed.

Televisions were tucked up against the ceiling all the way around the room, always playing sports events without sound, and the noise from the casino was a background noise, but not intrusive. So a player could actually hear a normal conversation at a table instead of having to shout as in some poker rooms.

This had always been my home casino, and even though I lived most of my time in Las Vegas, I loved being able to teleport to play here a few times a week. A completely different feeling than any Las Vegas poker room, that was for sure.

The Presumptive had to be no older than twenty-five, with dark short hair, black eyes, and almost white skin that he mostly kept hidden with long sleeves and a buttoned collar. From the looks of his rings, watch, and clothes, he had more money than he knew what to do with.

I had learned over the years that people with a lot of money sometimes, but not always, had great egos and a sense of entitlement.

I had a lot of money, and at times a large ego, especially at a poker table, but no sense at all of entitlement. I had earned every bit of my money and there would have been a time a decade or more ago I would never have sat down in a game this rich.

Tonight, I figured The Presumptive was going to entitle me to a large percentage of his money.

He ended up sitting at the other end of the table from me so I could see him directly.

He was brash and loud, but also had a level of uncertainty that he tried to hide with his brashness. He had also made a really, really stupid mistake by buying in with far too many chips.

I had bought in for two thousand. He had come to the table with five times that much in racks of chips. I was going to enjoy walking away from the table later on with those chips in racks.

After twice around the table, I had played no hands, just tossed all my cards away. But that allowed me to watch and get a good read on him.

He played fast and loose and tried to intimidate with his large stack of chips. And actually, in the right situation, that was a decent way to play, but not right off as a game started.

His second major mistake.

About half the table was made up of regular players in the room, all solid players, and they just sat back and stayed out of the guy's way as I did. A couple young kids from the Portland area mixed it up with him on a few early hands and both dinged a small amount out of the guy's stack, which made The Presumptive play even more aggressively.

The way to fight an overly aggressive player like him was to sit back and wait for a great hand and then play it weak and let him bet and then take his chips.

One hour into the game, I started to get a different read on idiot boy. He had started to become worried as he got down to about half his chips left in his stack.

I could sense the worry like it was a bad odor of a disease.

I knew that odor. It was addictive gambling odor and I had seen it more times than I ever wanted to think about on people in casinos.

And the more worried he got, the brasher he became, almost rude, and his play got more aggressive, which made his chips drop even faster.

When his chips got down to only two thousand left, he stood and moved to the cage and bought in for another ten thousand chips.

That was when it dawned on me he that he might not be actually playing on his own money, but had set up a line-of-credit with the casino. In other words, he had good credit and was playing with borrowed money.

A horrid thing to do and the way he got more worried, the credit might have been a sham of some sort or another.

After another hour, he was down another six thousand, about three of it sitting in front of me.

And numbers of tourists had cycled through the game, leaving their money before they left. All the regulars were just smiling because they had stumbled into a game made in heaven.

But The Presumptive almost stank from worry and addiction. To everyone else he kept it covered with brashness and sometimes just flat rudeness.

I needed to find out what was really going on.

TWO

I WAITED UNTIL the attention was distracted to the other end of the table and then froze time around me.

Actually, I didn't stop time, I just stepped between moments of time, but it had the appearance that I had frozen time.

Then I stood and said toward the ceiling, "Stan, need a little help."

Stan, my boss, the God of Poker, appeared a moment later.

He was dressed as he always dressed, in a button-down sweater, tan slacks, and brown loafers. With his plain face and short brown hair, he was the most nondescript person I had ever met. He liked to stay hidden.

On the other hand, I liked to be right out there. I always wore a black leather coat and a fedora-like black hat. I called it my superhero uniform.

When Stan appeared, I indicated the guy at the end. "Know him? He calls himself "The Presumptive."

Stan glanced at my large stacks of winnings and then laughed. "You must be in heaven playing with him."

"So never seen or heard of him before?" I asked.

Stan just looked at the guy a little more without answering. "He's playing scared. More than likely on borrowed money, even though he pretends to be rich with those rings and such. He's got an addiction problem."

Wow, my boss was good. No wonder he was the God of Poker. He could read a guy at a glance.

"My take on him exactly," I said. "This is a small casino and he might be getting this money on credit. I don't know, but he shows no signs of slowing down giving his money away."

"Think he's pulling a scam of some sort or another?" Stan asked.

"Can't figure it out though, whatever it is. Might just be a rich kid playing with parents' money, but I don't think so. I'm getting a sense of something more."

Stan nodded. "He might have just expected to win and sat down at the exact wrong table."

"He called himself The Presumptive so very possible," I said.

Stan stared at the guy for a moment, then asked, "Second buy in?"

"Second," I said. "Ten thousand both times."

Stan nodded and smiled at me like a parent looking at a child. "He will make three more rebuys, all ten grand. Take his money and let me know when you get it figured out. But don't let him leave the casino without calling me."

With that Stan vanished.

I was sure I could hear him laughing as I went back to my chair and got back into the flow of time.

Stan knew what was happening and he wanted me to figure it out.

How annoying.

Almost as annoying as idiot boy at the other end of the table.

Not quite, but close.

THREE

SO MUCH FOR my pleasurable game at my home casino while Patty worked. I focused in even more on both playing great cards and watching for any idea of what idiot boy was up to.

When he got down to two thousand in chips again, he went and rebought another ten thousand.

I now had a good nine thousand in front of me and the other four regulars who knew how to play against idiot boy's type of play had thousands each as well.

We were just plucking this guy like a dead chicken.

And his smell of fear and addiction just seemed to increase. I was amazed that no one around me could even smell it.

Finally, as he rebought for his fifth time, I couldn't take it any longer. If he was borrowing this money and planning on a scam, he was going to hit this casino for fifty thousand and that was too much.

I froze time again and jumped into the financial cage, something I almost never did.

They had his tab right on the counter clear as day. He had put fifty thousand in cash on deposit. He wasn't scamming the casino or playing on credit. It was his money and he had gone through it all, except for the chips in front of him on the table.

I jumped back to the table and let myself back into the flow of time.

With his last ten thousand on the table, I decided to try to engage him a little in conversation.

After he lost a fairly large pot to one of the regulars that idiot boy had kept raising over and over, I said to him. "Tough night, huh?"

He looked at me and shook his head. "My lot in life."

My little voice screamed at that answer. It wasn't the answer of a man fearful of losing, but a person resigned to his place.

"Looks like you can afford the loss," I said. "We all have them."

"I always have them," he said. "I'll go back, get more money, and then lose it again."

"So the nickname?" I asked as he shoved in his last two thousand in chips to cover a bet.

I was starting to understand. His nickname wasn't that he was the presumptive winner, but the presumptive loser.

"Just a joke for myself," he said, shaking his head.

"What's the punishment for?" I asked. "What did you do?"

As his last bit of money was pushed to another player, he looked at me and I think, for the first time, he finally saw me. He had been under some sort of screen to not be able to see me before he lost all his money.

And that screen had kept me from seeing him clearly as well. He now radiated power equal to that of a god.

A very old and powerful god.

Holy smokes, what had I just done?

He smiled at me and then shook his head. Then he looked up at the ceiling, all smell of worry and fear gone completely.

"Really?" he asked to the ceiling. "I mean, really?"

I took us both out of time and it didn't even startle him.

"Stan?" I said into the air. "We're done."

Stan appeared next to Laverne, Lady Luck herself. This guy really, really must be on the shit list if Laverne was here.

Laverne looked her normal stern self with a pinstriped business suit on and her hair pulled back tight off her face.

The guy stood up and joined the three of us standing near my end of the table.

"You going to be all right, Hermes?" Laverne asked, her face actually showing some compassion.

"Feeling fine again," he said, moving his shoulders around. "This treatment really works. Thanks."

The guy I had been calling silently idiot boy turned and shook my hand. "Glad I can remember that game," he said. "It was a pleasure playing with Poker Boy. I've heard so much about you. And you being able to spot me is really amazing."

I was just standing there feeling shocked. I had played a night of poker with one of the original gods of gambling, Hermes.

And kicked his ass.

And he wasn't angry.

Kicking a god's ass often resulted in great anger that resulted in earthquakes and lightning and all sorts of other really nasty stuff.

But for Hermes, the losing had clearly been a treatment of some sort.

"Thank you," I said. "But you had me worried."

Hermes nodded. "Yeah, this is sort of all my gambling addictions wrapped into one evening every five years or so. But by doing this, lancing the wound, so to speak, I don't need to gamble for another five years. A night like this just cleans me out."

"Makes Sally happy," Laverne said, smiling.

"That it does," Hermes said, laughing. "And never hurts to have the wife happy."

Clearly this Hermes was liked in his real, unprotected form.

At that moment, Patty appeared next to me. I hadn't realized how long the evening had taken and she was already off work and dressed in a casual blouse and jeans.

When she saw Stan and Laverne, she smiled and then turned to Hermes. "How have you been? How's Sally?"

My girlfriend knew Hermes. Holy smokes!

"She's doing great and going to be waiting for me to get home with a bottle of nice wine and a good dinner," Hermes said. "Thanks to your boyfriend here, I'm going to be early."

"Yeah," Patty said, laughing, "he can cause people to leave a poker table quickly."

"Not sure how to take that," I said.

Patty kissed my cheek. "In the best possible way."

And I had no idea how to take that, or the fact that everyone was laughing.

Hermes just patted my shoulder. "Poker Boy, you can help me with my treatment any time you want."

"Thanks," I said. "But I had no idea that you would be here tonight."

"So this was just happenstance?" he asked, shaking his head.

Hermes glanced back at all the stacks of chips in front of my position at the table and the stacks in front of the other regulars who had ridden this right down with me. "Certainly helps me understand that there are a lot better players in the world than I am. I think once every five years is enough."

With that he kissed Laverne's cheek, shook Stan's hand, hugged Patty, then shook my hand. "Let's get this back into real time so I can get out of here. I got dinner waiting."

"And you have a girlfriend waiting," Patty said to me, smiling. "I'll be home."

With that Patty and Laverne and Stan vanished.

As Hermes walked back to his seat, he laughed. "Looks to me, Poker Boy, that tonight, we are both winners."

I nodded. "In a far more important game than is played at this table."

"Got that right," Hermes said, smiling at me. "Totally right."

~

Can't Get Enough of
Poker Boy?

These stories and more are available at your favorite booksellers.

Now Available
from all your favorite booksellers
in trade paper and electronic editions.

USA Today Bestselling Writer
DEAN WESLEY SMITH
HERE TO STAY ON THE EDGE
Beautiful People
Have Their Issues Too

Stunningly beautiful Carol Lynn once again finds herself stood up on a blind date. A romantic patio, perfect warm evening, the smell of roasted duck in a thick cheese sauce, and a glass of red wine in her hand.

Perfect. If the bastard showed up. But the empty chair across from her spoke volumes.

Then the most handsome man she might ever dream about sat across from her. Not her date. And not in her league.

A sweet story of a romantic dinner. And a possible future.

HERE TO STAY ON THE EDGE

ONE

CAROL LYNN HADN'T given up on men just yet, but she was damned close.

The restaurant patio around her seemed to bustle with activity. The evening air was warm, but not too hot, the laughter from the dozen tables on the patio around her almost contagious.

The wonderful smell of what looked like a roasted duck in cheese sauce served to the couple at the table next to her made her stomach growl. She stared at her large glass of white wine for a moment, then took another sip and set it back down on the cloth covering the small round table.

She was alone in one of the most romantic settings in Portland, Oregon. The blue river moved slowly just beyond the patio, the sunset was lighting up the sky with bright shades of red and orange, and the bridge lights were just starting to come on, shining on the half-dozen bridges she could see from this restaurant.

Faint music played in the background, romantic music of some sort that she did not recognize, but would have liked under other circumstances.

Across from her an empty chair loomed as a stark reminder that she was being stood up, the empty wine glass in front of the chair a laughing reminder.

She was the only one alone at a table in this romantic setting.

Figured.

Story of her life.

The chair was supposed to have been filled by a man by the name of Stan. She had met him twice in the library where she worked, liked him, and he had seemed to like her.

With some major hints and her urging him on, he had finally got up his courage and asked her out, got a reservation and everything, and now was standing her up. Not even a phone call.

Nothing.

Again the story of her life when it came to men.

The bastard had better be dead or in the hospital because she wasn't listening to any other excuse. She had taken two hours to get dressed, put on a slight bit of makeup, something she never did, and then had spent another half hour just picking the right jewelry to go with her new light-blue summer dress.

The dress fit her figure perfectly and almost all the men on the patio had watched her enter.

At twenty-seven, she had three degrees, including two masters and was still as thin as she had been in college because she worked out every day. Her friends called her stunningly beautiful and were constantly trying to set her up.

And they were always stunned when it didn't work out, usually because the guy stood her up or left and never called after one date.

She didn't think of herself as beautiful because she had a slight Roman nose and her brown eyes were a little wide, but she had clear skin, a nice smile, long brown hair, and a decent figure, not too big in any area. She certainly should be able to attract a nice man.

Nope.

Nada.

Not even a loser of a man stuck around her.

So far her dates over the years, from high school onward, had all panned out quickly when she did manage to get a guy to even show up. The dates that did actually happen lasted only long enough for quick sex, and then the guy vanished into the hills without a word.

It had been consistent for as long as she had been trying to date. At some point, she just needed to accept that she was going to be alone for the rest of her life.

She sure couldn't figure out what she had been doing wrong.

But damn, tonight she was horny. At this point in her life, she would take a little quick sex with damn near anyone with a pulse. With that in mind for tonight, she had even gone so far as to buy expensive new sexy underwear, just in case the date got that far.

Nope.

As with most of the other dates in her past, it wasn't going to happen. Not even dinner was going to happen.

Bastard.

She glanced at her phone for the hundredth time to see if there was a message. None. And she had full bars.

She had been waiting now for almost an hour. That was enough for that jerk.

She would grab a pizza on the way home and a pint of chocolate Haagen-Dazs and spend the evening in front of her television with her cat Sam. She would have to do extra workouts the next few days to balance the calories, but at the moment she flat didn't care.

That was her routine when stood up and it had become familiar now, it had happened so many times.

She signaled for Paul, the waiter, to bring her check for the wine. He was an older man in his fifties with a quick smile, a large gut covered by a white apron, and no hair. When he did, she apologized for taking his table for an hour. She told him she had been stood up by a jerk.

"No problem," he said. "Sometimes things happen. You are a stunningly beautiful woman, there will be other dates."

"They mostly turn out this way," she said. "I think I am destined to be alone."

That seemed to surprise the man and he put her bill back down on the table, her credit card on top of it.

"Maybe you are destined to find the one man of your dreams," Paul said. "And other men know they will not fill that bill."

"Yeah, told myself that for years," she said, laughing and shaking her head.

"If you wouldn't mind," he said, "I have someone I would like you to meet."

"A blind date?" she asked. "I think after getting stood up, that might be a little much."

"He is not blind," Paul said, smiling. "But he is sitting at the bar and is a very nice man. Please stay for a moment. I will pay for your wine."

She started to object, but Paul had already turned and headed back inside the main part of the restaurant.

Why not? The wine was good, she had brand new sexy underwear on, she was in a restaurant and was hungry, and maybe, if this guy was sitting at a bar, he might be as horny and desperate as she was.

A horny man was better than a pizza and ice cream any day.

Even if he did vanish in the middle of the night.

TWO

IT MUST HAVE taken Paul a few minutes to convince his friend to come out onto the patio. Carol was about to head out and pay her tab at the front door when Paul came out of the restaurant, smiling.

Behind him was a Greek God, if Greek Gods wore a long dark coat that went all the way to the floor and a brown cowboy hat.

If they didn't they should.

Wow! Just wow!

The breath caught in her throat as she stared at the guy coming toward her behind Paul. His eyes were down, watching where he stepped as if he was embarrassed. He had a chiseled chin, sharp features under his hat, and a body that walked like an athlete.

He looked to be about six foot tall in his cowboy boots.

Carol forced herself to take a deep breath and glance around. Every woman on the patio was staring at the guy in the cowboy hat, some with their mouths open.

Oh, shit! Oh, shit! Oh, shit! What had she gotten herself into? This guy was way, way, way out of her league.

Paul indicated that the man in the long coat and cowboy hat should take the chair across from Carol.

Carol stood as the man took off his hat to reveal thick brown hair and brown eyes that seemed to see into her soul.

He just stared at her.

She stared back. If she didn't sit down pretty soon, her knees were going to give way.

"This is my nephew Ted from Idaho," Paul said.

Paul looked down at the credit card on her ticket to get her name. "Ted, this is Carol Lynn, I assume from here."

"I am," she said.

She managed to extend her hand and Ted shook it, sending electrical sparks through her entire body.

"Nice to meet you," he said, his voice deep and rich, a voice that fit his stunning good looks.

"The pleasure is all mine," Carol said.

"Sit, sit," Paul said.

Ted took off his coat and hat and handed them to Paul.

Ted was wearing an expensive dress shirt under the coat, tucked into his jeans, and he clearly had broad shoulders and muscles under that shirt.

"Thanks, Uncle Paul," he said.

"Dinner is on me," Paul said. "Drink up and look at the menu and I will return in ten minutes to take your order."

"You don't have to do that, Paul," Carol said.

"I do," he said. "No arguments."

He took Carol's card off the bill, put it on the table in front of her, picked up the bill and left.

Carol shook her head and looked back into the wonderful brown eyes of the most handsome man she had ever met sitting across from her. "Your uncle is a very nice man, but he doesn't need to buy us dinner."

Ted smiled, showing perfect white teeth. When he smiled, his face sort of lit up. Could the guy get any more perfect?

"Uncle Paul is very rich," Ted said. "So he can afford it. And besides, he owns this place and a dozen others around town."

"Why was he waiting tables?" she asked.

Ted just shook his head. "He does that at each of his restaurants twice a month. Says it keeps him in contact with his customers."

"Well, I am glad he does," she said, then felt herself blush a little, something she seldom did.

"As am I," Ted said, smiling and also blushing.

As they looked over the menu, the ice between them slowly broke as they compared dishes they liked and didn't like.

And after Paul took their order, they talked about Ted's business as a freelance electrical consultant, which is what had brought him to Portland and how he needed to stay for a few months.

And they talked about her job at the library and why she loved it so much and why her degrees had led her to the job.

All the while she talked, she couldn't believe the attraction she had for this man.

So finally, just to be clear, as they were both working on their salad course with bread that melted in her mouth, she asked the question she had been dreading.

"Are you married?"

He actually laughed and shook his head. "Not even close. I can't seem to get a woman to hang around long enough to even get to a second or third date."

"How is that possible?" she asked, staring at him.

"Uncle Paul told me you had been stood up," Ted said, laughing. "How is that possible? No sane man would ever not show up for a date with someone as beautiful as you are."

She could feel her face blushing again.

"That's why I agreed to come out here and have dinner with you," Ted said. "I know how hard it is to get stood up. It's happened to me more times than I can count."

She just stared at him, dumbfounded. He was fantastically handsome. Far, far out of her league.

So what woman was stupid enough to stand him up?

THREE

TED CHANGED THE subject to her exercise and for the next hour, through dinner and desserts, they talked and laughed.

She could not remember a time when she had enjoyed a dinner as much as the one tonight.

When they were finally sipping on an after-dinner wine that had to be more sugar than apricot flavor, Paul came back to their table. Over half the patio was now empty and there was a slight chill to the air that she hadn't noticed until now.

More than likely she had gone numb just talking to the incredible man across from her.

"All right," Paul said, "I'm going to put a stop to something for both of you right now."

She looked at him and frowned and she could see that Ted did the same thing.

"You two ever heard of the cheerleader effect?" Paul asked.

Ted shook his head, but Carol thought she knew. "In high school everyone assumes that a cheerleader is so popular and good looking, they always have dates, but they seldom do because everyone assumes that."

"Were you a cheerleader?" Ted asked.

"No," she said. "But I had no dates either."

"Exactly," Paul said. "So I have been watching you two enjoy each other's company for the night. Be honest, did you?"

Ted nodded. "Very much, thank you."

He looked at her when he said that and again she could feel her face getting slightly red. He was the only man she could remember that could get her to blush like that.

"Did you enjoy the meal as well and the company and conversation?" Paul asked her.

"Very, very much," she said, looking at Ted who glanced down at the table.

"So give me an honest answer, Ted," Paul said. "When you saw Carol here, did you think she was out of your league?"

"Way, way out," Ted said.

"That's exactly what I thought about you," Carol said, looking at Ted.

"So neither of you can imagine the other person staying with you for very long, right?" Paul asked.

Both of them nodded.

"So instead of letting the other person kick you out, you chicken out and leave or don't show up, as both your dates did tonight," Paul said.

"You were stood up as well?" Carol asked.

Ted again just nodded and looked at the wine glass in front of him.

"Your dates tonight," Paul said, "just couldn't handle the fear of being with someone they perceived to be way out of their league. So your dates took the easy way out."

"But I'm not out of anyone's league," Carol said. "I'm just a normal woman."

Paul shook his head and Ted actually laughed.

"You are so far from normal as to be frightening," Ted said. "You are the most beautiful woman I have ever had the pleasure to have dinner with."

She opened her mouth to say something, then just shut it. All thoughts were gone with that.

"And Ted here just thinks of himself as a regular guy," Paul said, "and flat doesn't understand why women run from him when he shows an interest."

"Because they think you are out of their league, so why try," Carol said, nodding. She was finally starting to understand where Paul was headed with this. If she had seen Ted in any other situation, she would have done the same thing and not even tried to get to know him because he was way out of her league.

Paul smiled. "You both have the cheerleader effect on people."

Paul stood and smiled. "Now talk it out, but I want to see you two together tomorrow night at my restaurant in the Pearl district. You each finally are with someone in the same league. Learn to believe it, would you?"

He turned away and Carol shouted at his back, "Thanks for a wonderful dinner."

Paul just waved an acknowledgement with one hand and vanished inside.

She looked back at Ted. "I'm having a very hard time believing you are interested in me."

He smiled. "I'm having a very hard time believing you are interested in me."

"So for both of us, we are in new waters," Carol said.

"I kind of think of it as standing on an edge," Ted said, smiling.

"And we can't make promises because neither one of us believe in them at the moment from the opposite sex," Carol said. "Right?"

"Exactly right," Ted said. "But I can tell you this: I want to be with you and it scares me to death."

"I want to be with you and you scare me to death as well," she said.

"So until we learn to trust that the other one won't chicken out and bail," Carol said, "we live on the edge."

"On the edge," he said, picking up his wine glass as a toast. "We're here to stay on the edge."

"I like that," she said, touching her glass to his. "To staying here on the edge."

She sipped the wonderful sweet wine, then set it down and looked at the man across from her. "Do you like forward women?"

He laughed, a laugh she would never get tired of hearing. "Damned if I know. Never met one."

"Well, you have tonight," she said, smiling at him.

"Then I like forward women," he said.

"Good," she said, "because I bought brand new sexy underwear yesterday and would love to show them to you right before you take them off of me."

He actually blushed slightly, but kept smiling. "I really, really, really do like forward women."

With that he stood and offered her his hand.

And she took it and it felt right, for the first time in her life.

Now Available
from all your favorite booksellers in trade paper and electronic editions.

USA TODAY BESTSELLING AUTHOR

DEAN WESLEY
SMITH

LAYING THE MUSIC
TO REST

A former college professor turned bartender, Doc finds himself trying to save his friends from a ghost under a lake in the wilderness of Idaho.

From diving into a ghost town buried under a lake to trying to stay alive on the sinking deck of the Titanic, this time-travel science fiction novel reads like a roller-coaster ride with all the twists and turns.

First published in paperback in 1989 from Warner Questar Books, Dean Wesley Smith's first published novel gives a lot of hints of his future series and his bestselling career spanning over a hundred and fifty novels.

Published here in its original form, without any changes, just as Dean wrote it almost thirty years ago.

LAYING THE MUSIC TO REST
Part 6

CHAPTER EIGHT

Boat Deck
First Cycle
April 15, 1912

THE TITANIC'S BAN, tucked back in an alcove beside the first-class entrance to the boat deck, played ragtime as the ship sank. Upbeat, happy music to cheer the passengers as they prepared to die.

It wasn't cheering me at all.

I didn't plan on dying just yet. I threaded a rope through the wooden slats of a chair, wrapped it around the legs of the other four chairs in the bundle, then yanked on it hard to pull all the chairs tightly together. Hard to believe I had been dumb enough to get into this. Going through the mirror had been a risk. I had known that. But I never expected anything like this. In all my forty years, I had never been this confused.

Or this scared.

Or this damn cold. The hair in my nose had frozen into needles the minute I stepped back out on the wood-covered boat deck. My ears ached, my knees were numb from kneeling, and I had lost track of any feeling in my fingers two minutes after starting this stupid raft.

I blew hard on my hands, then stuck them under my jacket to see if I could regain enough touch to tie the next knot. I didn't want to think about what would happen if the raft I was building didn't hold together. Or if Susan didn't come galloping to my rescue. I glanced around. Same thing as the last six hours. No sign of Susan and not a soul paying me the slightest bit of attention.

After getting jolted that first time by putting my hand through the maitre d', I had sat against the wall with my pack until I had calmed down enough to stand up without fear of a heart attack. Then I had gone looking for Susan, being real careful to not touch anyone. I did get one other jolt when a woman in a fur coat turned suddenly and would have bumped my arm, but for the fact that my arm went right through her. Again it felt as if I had brushed up against an electric fence. I couldn't imagine what running into some-one head-on would do. Probably be fatal.

I had spent the next few hours going through the halls, dining rooms, librar-ies, and card rooms, yelling for Susan. I had no idea how big the *Titanic* was until those hours. I wasn't able to cover even a quarter of the decks before there was an ugly rumbling noise deep in the ship and the engines stopped.

The *Titanic* had struck the iceberg.

That was the exact moment, as I felt the engines stop, and then listened to the huge stacks as they started blowing off the steam from the engines, that I decided I wasn't going down with the ship. I had the advantage of knowing what was going to happen and I could figure out a way to stay alive.

I had dragged my pack back up the stairs to the boat deck, only this time I went out on the port side and up about halfway to where there was a large supply of wooden deck chairs. I would build my own raft. Simple as that.

Only the intense cold wasn't making it so simple. I took a few shallow breaths and forced myself to try to relax and lis-ten to the music while my hands warmed.

The small, eight-man band stood fifty feet away on the *Titanic's* increasingly slanted boat deck. They were tucked out of the way in a shallow alcove formed by one of the ship's giant funnels and the entrance to the grand staircase. Their ghost white life jackets gave them a for-mal look as they stood with their backs to the wall and played to the dark Atlantic night.

They had played right through the madness that had filled the boat deck during the boarding of the lifeboats. There was no doubt they were damn good musicians, but I didn't know how they could play in this extreme cold. I could barely tie a rope, let alone finger an instrument. Yet they had played for what seemed like hours, starting in the first-class lounge, then moving outside on the boat deck. Amazing sense of duty. Legend had it they played right to the final moments. Not one of them sur-vived. It looked like I was about to find out how true that legend was.

I blew on my hands again. My fingers felt like blocks of wood. There wasn't even enough feeling left for them to hurt. I was getting too damn old for this.

I should have listened to Dean Haycraft and stayed on at the university. At least my office had been warm. Boring, but warm.

I studied the makeshift raft I had been frantically building as the bow of the ship sank deeper and deeper into the calm, black water. I had figured that if I tied wooden deck chairs in bundles five thick, then tied four bundles together, I might have something that would hold me and my backpack out of the ice-cold Atlantic water. It only had to stay afloat for three hours. If I remembered right, the *Carpathia*, the *Titanic's* rescue ship, would arrive by then. I didn't want to think about the chance that they wouldn't be able to see me either. I'd face that problem when I got to it.

The raft didn't look like much, but it might make the three hours. Assuming, of course, that I could get the raft over the railing and drop it into the water without it breaking apart, then paddle it far enough away from the *Titanic* that the suction from the huge ship going under wouldn't pull both me and the raft with it. Damn big assumptions to be gambling my life on.

It didn't much matter now. In a few minutes, I wouldn't have a choice. The slant of the deck had become far more pronounced and water now rolled over the bow of the ship. The huge ship was about to stand on its nose and unless something pulled my ass out of here real soon, the raft was going to be my only hope.

I yanked another length of rope free from a discarded lifeboat cover and wound it tightly around the chair legs of one bundle, then in through the seating slats of another. Fifteen hundred people would drown or die from exposure in the next few hours. Yet, as far as I could see,

I was the only one building a raft. There was certainly no shortage of rope with all the lifeboat covers tossed aside, and there had to be two hundred deck chairs on this side of the boat deck alone. But not one of the hundreds of passengers left on the boat deck was even tossing chairs into the water. They all just climbed slowly toward the stern of the ship like a death march, making no attempt to save themselves. Made no sense. Hell, nothing on the *Titanic* made sense.

The band finished their song and started another ragtime tune. I glanced down the deck where they played. I hadn't noticed before, but at least two dozen people now stood listening to them, leaning against the rail or standing in small groups. None of the listeners wore life preservers. It was as if they were simply watching a band in their local park on a Sunday afternoon.

Damn strange. Everywhere I looked there were questions. Where had Susan gone? Why had I ended up on the *Titanic*? Why weren't more people trying to save themselves? How the hell was I going to get back home? Questions. Questions. Questions. Not an answer in sight. And no time to do any more looking.

I blew on my hands again, then worked at stacking the last bundle of folded chairs. Maybe I'd tie just one more chair on top of each bundle just to make sure. I'd have to—

"You're wasting your time, you know."

I hadn't heard or seen her come up, so her sudden declaration startled me and I banged together the chairs I was stacking, sending one clattering down the sloped deck.

She stood over me like a teacher over a naughty child. She wore a high-necked black evening gown, elbow-length black gloves, and a small, fashionable black hat perched nestlike on her dark brown hair. I guessed her age to be about thirty-five. She took a sip of a golden liquid from a cordial glass and smiled.

I didn't know what I was more surprised by: what she was wearing, her complete calmness, or that she had spoken to me.

Suddenly, after six hours of saying "pardon me," or "excuse me," or yelling and getting nothing for my troubles but a jolt of electricity, here was this lady talking to me and damned if I could think of anything to say.

"Aren't you cold?" I finally asked, going for the easy question first and indicating her thin dress.

"Do you like it?" she asked, turning a half-turn one way, then back, like a young girl in front of a mirror. "I found it especially for the party. I think it was one of Mrs. Straus's." As she spoke, her breath crystallized in front of her face, glowing in the deck lights and giving her a ghostlike appearance.

"It's striking, but don't you think it a might thin for the weather we're having?" To illustrate my point, I blew on my hands in a futile effort to get some feeling back in them.

She shrugged. "After a few years, you get used to it."

"Few years?" What the hell did she mean by that?

She flashed a smile that made me wish I wasn't about to die, then took another sip from her glass.

I studied my raft and tried to think. Maybe it would hold us both. I could throw a few more chairs over the side and stack them on top of the raft to make up for the extra load. That might make the raft a little top-heavy, but she seemed light enough. Besides, she could help me get the raft over the rail and away from the ship.

"You're new on board, aren't you?" she asked. "This your first cycle?"

"Damned if I know first from last," I said, gathering up the extra chairs and stacking them on top of my raft. "But I've been here about six hours." I wrapped the rope around the chair legs to keep the chairs from scattering.

She laughed softly. "I thought so. Only newcomers do things like this." She indicated the raft. "It's probably quite workable, but—"

"Just what's so wrong with a person saving their own skin?" I demanded. "I don't see you doing anything."

"I don't need to," she said. "Neither do you. Really we don't." She pointed down the slanted deck at the band. They had finished another ragtime song. "That was their last full song. We recycle fifteen seconds after they start 'Autumn.'"

Now Available
from all your favorite booksellers
in trade paper and electronic editions.

As if she were their leader, the band raised their instruments and began playing "Autumn."

"By the way, my name is Marjorie. Marjorie Thiel. I'm from New Mexico. 1972." She leaned down and extended a black-gloved hand.

I didn't know whether to touch her or not. I doubted if my heart could take many more of those shocks. I decided I didn't really have much to lose at this point.

"Kellogg Jones." I said as I shook her soft, warm hand. "Idaho. 1990. Everyone calls me Doc."

Her soft laugh sent breath crystals swirling in the light from the draped windows. "Tell you what, Mr. Doc. You meet me in the first-class smoking lounge in thirty minutes and I'll fix you a drink. You do drink, don't you?"

I nodded. "But—"

"Good," she said, and took a sip from her glass. "Thirty minutes. I do so love current news." She turned and started down the slanted wooden deck toward the band. I watched her for a moment, amazed that she could keep her footing in such high heels.

She was between steps when everything faded, exactly as it had when I triggered the mirror at the lodge.

Then I was in the blackness again.

No up or down. No light. No sound. No smells.

Nothing. The same feeling of total emptiness as six hours before.

It lasted long enough for me to wonder where I would end up this time. Barely. Then the lights came back up like a curtain on the second act of a play.

I was again standing in the officer's promenade section on the starboard side of the *Titanic's* boat deck. Wind carried

the salt spray up into my face as the huge ship raced through the gray waters. The sky was splattered with streaks of red as the sun again set on the *Titanic's* last night.

Everything was the same as it had been six hours before.

Exactly.

I had a full stomach from Constance's dinner, the heavy pack was on my back, and I wasn't wearing my coat. On top of that, I was warm. Warm from sitting in the lodge's big living room.

Had the last six hours been a dream? Or was I really standing here again?

I laughed a strained laugh into the cold North Atlantic wind. And I thought I had been confused the first time around.

CHAPTER ELEVEN

First-Class Lounge
Second Cycle
April 14, 1912

THIRTY MINUTES AFTER I found myself starting my six hours on the *Titanic* all over again, Marjorie Thiel walked through the aft door of the first-class lounge. She was wearing black slacks, a silk blouse, and a long strand of pearls. Her thick brown hair was pulled back and tied with a white ribbon and she smiled when she saw me. I liked her smile.

It had been a long thirty minutes for me, waiting and wondering if she would appear. After I had gotten my bearings again and talked myself into realizing I really *was* back on the boat deck in the same place I had arrived, I eased the pack to the deck and then dragged it over and leaned it against the bulkhead. As I had the first time, I had unwrapped my ski parka from around the rifle, covered the rifle with a pair of pants, then put on the parka. In a daze, I had gone over to the railing and stood, staring out over the ocean while trying to make sense out of what was going on around me.

I hadn't gotten past the first twenty questions when behind me a door in the bulkhead opened with a loud clang and two men came out and turned toward the entrance to the grand staircase. One wore a turtleneck sweater and the other a ship's uniform. They were the same two men who had almost run into me six hours earlier. Only this time I was standing farther up the deck as they repeated their exact motions, ducking under the rope barrier, going inside and down the stairs. I felt as if I were watching a movie I had just seen, only from a different seat in the theater.

It appeared I was about to repeat the same six hours. But this time I would get to do different things while the ship and its crew stayed on their original course.

I followed the two men inside and spent the rest of the thirty minutes standing near the bow entrance to the first-class lounge, leaning against an oak column, and watching the passengers.

When Marjorie finally came through the stern door, I acknowledged her smile with a slight wave, then moved across the room to meet her. Most of the room was now empty. The two men I had followed down to the dining room the first time around had already left, passing me as I stood beside the door.

Marjorie pointed toward a booth under a port-side window and I headed there as she seated herself.

"Pretty shocking, isn't it?" she said as I got to the booth. No hello, how are you. Nothing.

"What's that?" I studied her face as I slid into the booth across from her. She was a much more striking woman in the light than she had been outside in the cold Atlantic night. I reduced my estimate of her age by a year or so, and even that might have been a little high. She had intense green eyes and lots of smile lines in her face. I liked her right off.

"All this," she said, sweeping her arm around at the lush room and the furnishings that by 1990 standards would have cost a fortune. "Being on the *Titanic*, time repeating itself over and over."

"Time doing what?" She ignored my question and went right on.

"I'm new enough on board that I remember how shocking it can be the first few times. Not like some of those rude ones who were on deck listening to the music. They were laughing at you. That's why I went up to talk to you."

"I'm glad you did," I said. "But I don't understand why they were laughing. I was—"

She held up her hand. "Lots of time for that. I promised I'd make you a drink. What would you like?" She slid out of the booth and stood waiting for my answer.

After the last six and a half hours, I felt I needed something strong. Real strong. "Scotch. Rocks. Splash of soda, if you can."

She laughed. "Practiced drinker, huh?"

"Bartender," I said. "Mind if I tag along?" I really wasn't a practiced drinker like the scotch implied. I used to drink scotch a lot, but I hadn't had one since the month after Carla died in that car wreck. Of course, during that month right after the funeral I had drunk a lot of it while trying to forget. The scotch hadn't helped.

"Sure," she said, turning and heading across the lounge's plush carpet toward the oak bar built into the center wall. "Just be careful of the passengers and crew. In case you haven't noticed yet, touching one of them gives you a real jolt."

"I noticed," I said. "Twice."

"Don't worry. After a few years you know exactly how they're all going to move, right down to who's going to pick their nose when. You get real good at avoiding them. Mostly the prisoners stay in areas where there aren't too many passengers."

"Years? Prisoners?" My voice must have sounded as shocked as I felt. The full reality of being stuck on the *Titanic* for years was finally starting to hit me. I didn't want to think about what she meant by prisoners.

"That's right," she said softly. "What was the date before you got pulled here?"

"June twenty-ninth, 1990."

I was cleaning my grandmother's hand mirror on August third, 1972, and found myself here. Almost eighteen years at four cycles a day. How many would that be?" She stared off at the ceiling trying to figure the math, then gave up. "I never was any good at math. You'd better stay here and watch how I do this. I know how this guy moves." She laughed. "I ought to. I drink here often enough."

I stood near the entrance as she ducked around behind the ornate oak and maple bar and moved toward the well. She waited for a few moments until the bartender, a man in his early forties, draped his bar towel over his shoulder and moved down the bar. Marjorie stepped into position at the well and, with practiced ease, pulled two crystal rocks glasses off the overhead rack, scooped ice into both, filled one with a brand of scotch I didn't recognize, and then filled the other with what looked to be a brandy. She then grabbed a bottle of soda out of the area below the ice and added a touch to mine.

She had my drink in my hand before the bartender even stopped walking away.

"Fast," I said, holding my drink up with a nod of thanks.

"Bartender," she said, smiling. "Flagstaff for a few years, then Vegas. I was back in Flagstaff helping with my grandmother's estate when I was pulled here."

I followed her back over to the same booth under the port-side windows. Through the paned window was the first-class promenade and beyond that the dark waters of the North Atlantic. I slid over the cloth seat of the booth until I had my back to the water. I'd have to face that again soon enough.

"Where'd you work?" she asked after a sip of her drink.

"Boise. A place I half owned called the Garden. Taught at the university before that."

"Professor type, huh?" She laughed.

"That's why the name Doc. Too damn many degrees."

Again she laughed. She seemed to be the type of woman who enjoyed life. Every time she laughed, her face would almost glow. Infectious. I found myself relaxing around her.

"So, Mr. Doc. Tell me what you were doing when you ended up here?"

"Being stupid, from the looks of things."

"Huh?" she said, stopping in the middle of a sip of brandy and looking up at me.

"I came here on purpose."

"You did *what*?" She shouted the last word and I glanced around the room to see if anyone noticed. Of course, no one did. "Why would you do that? I don't understand how you even knew. No one I've talked to has come here on purpose."

It was my turn to laugh. "I didn't know where I was heading. Not really. I was following someone who triggered the mirror right before I did and might be here. You seen any other newcomers besides me? A woman with short, white hair named Susan?"

Marjorie shook her head. "You're the first new person I've seen in the last six months. But that doesn't mean anything. It's a big ship. I can't believe anyone would come here purposefully. Do you have a way out?"

"That's exactly what I'm starting to hope Susan has."

Marjorie had put her glass down and was staring intently across the table at me. "For God's sake, would you tell me how you got here?"

"Sure, if you promise to answer some questions for me when I'm done."

"Deal," she said and we shook hands on it. Her hand was warm and smooth and I didn't want to let it go for fear she too would simply vanish. But I did and she settled back into the soft seat.

I spent the next forty-five minutes going over the story about the lodge and about the ghost named Gretchen. I told her about Constance and Fred and about how much the lodge meant to them. I told her about Susan and her strange story about this being a group collected by some unknown people she called Seeders to give mankind a second chance after humanity pulled the plug on itself. That part sounded stupid the minute I said it, but at least Marjorie was nice enough not to laugh.

Then I found myself telling her about how bored I had been teaching and how dull it was in the bar and how stagnant my life had become. Admitting that part to her surprised me. I ended my story with the weak rationale that I came through the mirror to look for the ghost's lost lover. She didn't laugh at that one either, which meant she was a nicer person than I had hoped.

Some Classic Dean Wesley Smith Stories
Available at your favorite booksellers.

"You need another drink?" I asked at the end of my story.

"Sure thing," she said. We crossed the distance over the thick, patterned carpet to the bar in silence.

"What will it be?" This time I went around behind the bar while she stayed at the edge.

"Brandy," she said. "You'll find it to the left. The scotch is above it." The main bartender was standing down the bar talking to one of the waiters.

I watched him out of the corner of my eye as I grabbed two rocks glasses off the rack and filled them. I stayed with the same scotch she had poured for me. It had tasted good after the first sip or so. A light, smoky taste that I knew I could grow to like very quickly.

"How come he can't see the glasses move?" I said as I slid her drink across the end of the bar. "It's obvious we're invisible to them, or something like that. But shouldn't he be able to see the glasses move?"

She shrugged. "They can't. I don't know why. I remember someone theorizing it had to do with us touching it. And them being locked into exactly what happened in their time frame. Something about solidarity of time. Or something like that."

She shrugged and tasted her drink. "I don't know how it all works, but it works for everything. In fact, I'm wearing a passenger's clothes right now." She indicated her blouse and pearls as we headed back toward the booth. Before she sat down she pointed at her slacks. "A man's pants. I was in my bathrobe when I arrived and every six hours I end up back in my bathrobe."

"Where? I didn't see you anywhere on the boat deck when I came through."

She laughed. "I end up down on E deck near the engineer's mess. Gave me a real start the first few times, let me tell you."

"I know the feeling."

Her face went serious again. "You think this Susan's story is true?"

"When I saw her pop out of that chair, I started thinking it just might be. And after the last few hours, I don't know what to think. Someone or something has a reason for setting this up. What little bit she told me makes as much sense as anything else I can think of."

Marjorie nodded. "Then she's probably here somewhere. And if she knew what she was getting into, she wouldn't do all the newcomer's stuff that would make her stand out."

"Like building a raft?" I said.

"Like building a raft." She touched my arm. I really enjoyed the light feel of her fingers. "At least you tried to save yourself. I went down to the main first-class dining room and threw plates at people to try to get someone to talk to me. It's real unnerving to watch a plate hit someone in the side of the head and not even have them flinch."

I laughed. "I can imagine. I tried and failed to get someone to listen to me a few hours ago. How about answering some of my questions, now?"

"What I can," she said.

I looked across the table at her. There were so many questions, I didn't know where to start. And the funny thing was that even though I was so confused, I found myself wanting to ask her questions about her life and what she liked and didn't like. And if she had been married.

I forced my thoughts back on questions that had been plaguing me the last seven hours and picked the first one that came to mind. "From what I've gathered, you've been on this ship since 1972. Right?"

She nodded.

"And every six hours you find your-self back in your bathrobe in the same place you started. Correct?"

"I'm afraid so."

"And you can remember all of the six hours before?"

Again she nodded. "Our minds remember, but our bodies don't."

"I don't understand," I said. "How can your body not remember?"

"I don't know how it works. But our bodies repeat. I still look exactly how I did when I arrived here in 1972. Same number of gray hairs. Same exact wrin-kles. Everything. I've talked to people who look twenty and have been here fifty years."

"Back up a minute. You mean we don't age?"

She nodded. "That's right. And if you were hungry when you came through, even if you eat right before the cycle, you're hungry again." She laughed. "There's a guy named Greg who was drunk when he was pulled here. Every six hours he's drunk again." She laughed again and I couldn't help but join her. "He's hungover four times a day and he's been here longer than I have."

That would explain why I had been warm and full again on the boat deck after being so cold moments before while building the raft. And if what she said was true, then it was possible that Alex might still be alive, and looking exactly like he had in 1909.

"So everyone who was ever brought here is still here?"

"Afraid not. Quite a few flip out and kill themselves, or go over the side and drown before they cycle. Death stops the cycle. So far, it has been the only way to escape the *Titanic*. However, the good side is that if you're injured, you come back healthy the next cycle."

I took a long sip of my scotch and let the chills from that news finish doing their tap dance along my spine.

"So how many people like us are there?"

"We call ourselves the *Titanic* pris-oners. Last time someone tried to count, there were over four hundred. There could be more, though. That was a few years back."

"Where are they?" I fanned my arm at the almost empty lounge.

"Everywhere. In case you didn't notice, this ship is huge. There are over two thousand original passengers and crew, and not even close to all the rooms are full. In fact, someone did some figur-ing once and came up with the fact that the first-class section was only half-full and second class was closer to only one-third full. Lots and lots of room. Most of us prisoners stay in the cabins and just sleep or read. Especially at the beginning of the cycle when most of the passengers are out and about. Another hour or so, when the passengers start turning in for the night, more prisoners will be wander-ing around. Then, when the ship hits the iceberg, we all go back into hiding until the next cycle. Unless, of course, there is a party like there was last cycle."

I sipped my drink and tried to scram-ble my thoughts into some sort of form. Impossible task. The more I saw what I had gotten myself into, the less I wanted to know. And the more I wanted to find Susan and figure out a way off this doomed ship.

"You know," she said. "Hearing that there might be a purpose to all of us being here sort of feels nice. All these years, I've been going along hoping that I would get back in time to see my mother alive and thinking this was all some big joke or dream I was going to wake up from and laugh at. But if that woman's story is true, and we're the ones to start over for mankind, that adds a reason for living. Know what I mean?"

I nodded. I was starting to. Three days ago I would have laughed at her and called the idea of starting humanity over a wish-fulfillment dream. But after yesterday and the last few hours, I had a much more open mind. But I couldn't imagine the boredom of being on the same ship for years and years. I didn't like the thought of having to completely start over every six hours. I'd only been on board eight hours and I knew I couldn't understand what she felt.

But she looked like she wanted to help. And help was what I needed. "Think you might want to see if we can find Susan, if she's on board? And maybe this Alex guy while we're at it?"

"I'd love to." She smiled at me with a smile I knew would stick in my memory for a long time. All the years since Carla died I'd never found anyone who interested me even in the slightest. Now I'd met someone who just might, and it was on a sinking ship. Figured.

"Then let's get going," I said as I downed the rest of my scotch and slid the glass into the center of the linen-covered table. "It's your turn to pour. Only this time make it a vodka soda with a squeeze. That scotch tastes just a little too good."

"Ask and you shall receive," she said, standing and heading for the bar.

I followed along behind her, hoping it was going to be that simple.

~

Some Classic Dean Wesley Smith Stories
Available at your favorite booksellers.

USA Today Bestselling Writer
DEAN WESLEY
SMITH
She Took And Took
Until He Said, "No More."
AN OBSCENE CRIME
AGAINST PASSION

James Ward no longer cares what his wife does in her spare time. He no longer cares about anything, actually.

Deborah took his passion over years. Drained him until he could give no more.

But on Bryant Street, sick relationships often reveal hidden secrets.

Passion functions as a food for some, energy for others. But who knows what role passion plays on Bryant Street.

AN OBSCENE CRIME AGAINST PASSION
A Bryant Street Story

ONE

The night James Ward finally confronted his wife for what she truly was started when police car lights flashed outside the large picture window of his suburban home. The drawn cloth curtains kept most of the light out, as well as the closed blinds under the curtains, but he still noticed the blue-red combination.

He couldn't remember the last time he had opened those windows and unless he heard shots out there in the cul-de-sac, he wasn't opening them now. The last baseball games before the All-Star break were being played tonight and he wanted to make sure he caught as many of them as he could.

He glanced around at his two-bedroom ranch-style home from his favorite recliner wondering where Deborah had gone. Over the last few years they had just drifted into doing their own things in their own ways at their own times.

The marriage had become convenient for both of them, passion a thing of the past, as he had expected would happen when they married but had hoped would not happen, as any newlywed hopes.

His life now was working at the insurance agency and watching baseball and doing a little betting on games down at the local casino. And just waiting. He did not expect his wait to end right before the All-Star Break in baseball.

He honestly had no idea what Deborah's interests had become as they drifted apart. She said she did some teaching, but he didn't remember what type or when or where.

And he honestly didn't care. Sad, considering she was his wife.

James was a tall, handsome man, at least many said that, and did some minor exercise to stay in shape. Deborah was just as stunningly beautiful now as the day he met her.

Everyone who saw them together said they made a perfect couple.

If they only knew.

Suddenly, just as the two teams were returning to the field after the seventh inning to finish up the nine-one disaster-of-a-game he had been watching, a loud banging at the front door shook the house.

"Deborah!" he shouted.

No response.

More banging.

"All right, all right," he said, climbing out of his recliner and heading for the door.

On the front porch stood two police officers. One a man, one a woman. The woman cop had a hooker by the arm and the hooker was turned away from the porch light.

He had no idea why cops would bring a hooker to his door at eight in the evening on a weeknight.

The cops were dressed in standard city cop uniforms and the hooker had on a very, very short skirt that barely covered the bottom of her ass, a mesh blouse that you could see through, torn black stockings, and heels so high that they looked more like stilts than shoes.

Women like her often walked along some of the worst streets downtown. He always avoided those areas. He just wasn't interested.

"You James Ward?" the guy asked.

"Yeah," James said.

"You married to Deborah Ward?" the guy asked.

"I am," James said. "Is she all right?"

"She seems to be," the cop said, handing James a small purse. "But might want to get her some help."

"And keep her off the streets," the woman cop said. "Dangerous downtown."

With that, the woman cop turned the hooker around and pushed her toward the door.

The hooker nodded to James and walked past him into the house, taking the small purse out of his hands as she went.

The cops both nodded to James without smiling and turned back toward their car as James stood there, surprised that the night had finally arrived.

It seemed events had transpired to move his life forward.

Finally, he slowly backed into the house and closed the door.

Then he turned around.

Deborah, his wife of five years, dressed like a twenty-dollar streetwalker, stood there, facing him. Her makeup was almost so thick as to crack and her normally wonderful brown hair had been greased back off her face.

"Surprise, huh?" she said, then popped some gum.

He opened his mouth, but said nothing.

Nothing.

"Let me go take a hot shower, get into my normal costume, and then we can talk," she said. "Be a sweetie and fix me a Bloody Mary. All the fixings are in the cabinet above the fridge where you would never look. It was a bitch of a night out there."

With a practiced ease on the extremely tall heels, she turned and headed back toward her closet and bedroom.

All James could do was stand there and watch her ass sway under her tight, short skirt as she went down the hall. That was an amazing costume she was wearing.

Then he went over and turned off the game and headed for the kitchen.

With this, he was going to need a drink as well.

Maybe two. If the night turned out as he hoped it would.

TWO

THE KITCHEN OF their suburban home was everything Deborah had wanted when they moved in. White modern cabinets, granite countertops, a dark floor, and modern stainless appliances.

The entire house had been remodeled. Some of it to her wants, a lot to his hidden reasons.

On the way to the kitchen he clicked a few hidden switches that would help him with the evening to come.

The kitchen table was custom-made to fit the space and could hold six, but since neither of them had much in the way of friends, that table had usually seated only the two of them. And their formal dining room had never been used.

Just wasn't either of their styles or their natures to have friends.

James hadn't objected to anything she had added in the remodel as long as it made her smile. When they were first married five years ago, he had loved to see her smile.

She had been fun to watch.

And they had made love regularly, in all sorts of ways. He liked that more than he wanted to admit.

That had ended slowly over the first year.

James dug out the glasses, the Bloody Mary mix, the vodka, and even a couple sticks of celery from the fridge he hadn't noticed before. He normally drank beer and didn't much like vegetables.

He put her drink in front of her chair and sat down in his chair and sipped on his drink, stirring it with the celery.

Since he had spent so much time at the casino lately in the sports book, he and Deborah had taken to eating meals on their own.

Now that he thought about it, the only thing they had left in their marriage was this house. Wow, that was sad.

But it felt more like a fact to him than a sadness. He had hoped for something more. Sure.

But it hadn't happened.

Shouldn't he be angry at all this? At her hooking downtown? At her sleeping with who knew how many other men?

A normal husband would.

He tried to think back. He couldn't remember the last time he had gotten angry about anything. It had been a very long time.

He didn't even get that much of a thrill with winning a bet and didn't get angry either with losing. Gambling used to make him feel alive.

Wow, he had become a dead shell in this marriage. How pathetic was that?

He needed new energy, new focus, new everything. Looked like after tonight he was finally going to get it.

After a few minutes, Deborah came out wearing her blue bathrobe and slippers. Her hair was wet and pulled back and her face looked like it had been scrubbed pretty well to get the makeup off.

She didn't even look close to the same woman who had walked through the front door thirty minutes ago. This was the Deborah he had married.

She sat down and took a pretty good drink of her Bloody Mary, then sat back with a sigh.

"Thanks, I needed that."

He nodded and took another drink as well.

Then he looked at her. "How long have you been doing this?"

She laughed. "If you mean being a prostitute, since I was fifteen. I was trained by my mother."

Again his mouth opened and yet not a word came out.

Nothing.

There was just nothing he could say to that as her husband.

Finally, he just shook his head and took another sip of his drink. A normal husband with a normal wife would be furiously angry at all this, at being lied to, at everything.

But he wasn't.

He couldn't be and he actually didn't feel a thing, as she knew would be the case.

She stared at him for a moment, then seemed to finally take pity on him, as he had been hoping for five years she would do.

"Have you ever met a person who just seemed to suck the life out of a room?" she asked.

He nodded. "Numbers of them back in college. There is a guy by the name of Hank in our office that does the same thing at times."

"You ever wonder where that life goes?" she asked.

He looked into her deep brown eyes and could see her question was serious. She was going to finally tell him the truth.

About damned time. Way too late, however.

"You ever heard of vampires?" she asked.

He nodded.

"Vampires in fiction survive from taking the life force, blood, out of others."

He nodded. He had seen his share of bad movies.

"Blood vampires do not exist," she said, matter-of-factly, looking at him and seeming to hold him.

"But energy eating beings do exist," she said. "They are ancient humans that need the energy, the passion, the life force of normal humans to exist. I am one of them. We call ourselves Primals."

The truth was finally out.

Finally.

The cop had been right, she really did need help. Just not the help the cop had intended.

"Have you been wondering why you feel nothing anymore about anything and are not angry right now about your wife being a hooker?"

He nodded, going with her. "That has bothered me."

"I keep you drained of that sort of energy," she said. "It's why you took that dull job, bet on sports without any thrill of winning or worry about losing, and why we stopped having sex a long time ago."

"You keep me drained?" he asked. "Why would you do that?"

"Because for the next fifteen or twenty years, I needed what we Primals call a cow. You, my sweet James, are my cow."

Damn he wanted to get angry, but just nothing came up.

"What exactly is the function of a cow?" he asked.

"I will not age," she said, "so for the next fifteen or so years, until our age difference starts to get noticed, you will supply me with a base level of energy, passion, joy, enough for me to survive for weeks at a time without being around others."

She was taking his joy, his energy, his caring, as he knew she was. As he had known it from the moment he tracked her down and got close to her, let her feel his energy.

"So why are you hooking?" he asked, sipping on his Bloody Mary.

"Once a week I need the boost, the thrill of sex with strangers, the fear that goes with that sex, the passion of men not used to feeling passion."

"You drain them all?" he asked.

"In a matter of speaking," she said, smiling. "Yes. They feel empty, calm, and without guilt when they leave me."

"So why me?" he asked.

He knew the answer. But now that her truth was out in the air between them, he wanted to hear her say it.

She smiled at him. A cold smile as only a Primal can give, but a real smile.

"Because I love you," she said. "And I wanted to spend a couple decades with you."

"Until I die from lack of energy," he said.

She nodded. "Pretty much."

He knew that wasn't going to happen. And it really made him sad to hear her say that. He had hoped for a different result.

"So are you going to keep hooking?" he asked. "That seems like a rather risky thing to continue to do after tonight, now that your name is on file with the police."

He was actually very glad she had slipped up and her name was on file as a hooker. It would make the next things he had to do even easier.

"I was thinking we need to have your brother come live with us," she said. "We have two spare rooms. Maybe he and his wife could both come. That would be fun for me."

He looked at her, knowing exactly what she was planning, but still playing along. "I don't have a brother."

"Of course you don't," she said, laughing. "I'll find us one, maybe a couple, and get us a cover story. It will be far more fun for a few years than walking those streets in those heels."

He just shook his head. So now he was going to share Deborah with two other people.

It seemed time to end this.

He sipped on his Bloody Mary, then looked up at her and smiled. "Ever hear of a group called Libertas?"

Her face drained of the freshly-washed look. Her eyes darted from one side to the other, clearly looking for a way to run.

There was no way.

He had made this house a perfect Primal trap and he had turned on that trap while she was in the shower.

"You didn't answer my question," he said.

"Libertas is a group of hunters that survive on finding and draining Primals such as myself."

She looked at him, really looked at him. "Are you a Libertas?"

"Of course I am," he said, laughing. "When I saw you that first day we met in the supermarket, your arrogance of just brushing men and draining them, I knew I could easily convince you I could be a perfect cow."

Her eyes flashed in anger. But then that anger faded and her skin got pale.

He sipped on his Bloody Mary as she slowly realized what was happening to her. He was draining her energy into the fields surrounding the house. And the house was then feeding him that energy through his chair.

She tried to stand, to run, but it was too late. She didn't have the energy left in her body for even that much.

A couple hundred years ago, he would have had to fight and kill her in a bloody fashion, cutting off her head and everything.

But with the modern science at his disposal, he could build a trap that would pull the energy from her.

A lot better than cutting off her head.

"How did you keep yourself hidden from me?" she asked, her voice weakening.

"Your arrogance," he said. "You never thought to look and I played your cow perfectly, didn't I? When a hunter starts to believe they cannot be beat, then the hunted have a clear advantage."

She could no longer hold up her head and she slumped to the table.

He could see her clear, wonderful skin start to wrinkle and become brittle just as if she were an old woman.

"And just so you know," he said. "I loved you as well. And if you hadn't wanted me to be your cow, we could have had a great and long life together."

She didn't have the energy to say anything, but she did acknowledge that she had heard him by raising a few fingers.

He sat back, sipping his Bloody Mary, letting the energy she had in her body pour through the house and into him. For the first time in years, he again felt alive.

He had won the fight and another Primal would soon be gone from the planet. And that was worth a drink over.

He kept sipping on his Bloody Mary, watching as his wife of five years shrunk up more and more.

She now no longer had the capability to even move.

Her energy that was pouring through the house to him would keep him alive for decades to come. Because just as Primals, Libertas also were immortal. Only they did not feed off the helpless, they fed from Primals.

He had been doing so for more centuries than he wanted to remember.

She never knew in five years that while she was taking surface, human energy from him, he was pulling deeper energy from her. More than likely that was why she had decided to go find others. She didn't get enough from him because he took almost as much from her as she took from him.

It had been a perfect balance.

Many would say a perfect marriage.

Finally, her body broke apart, mostly into dust as the house kept sucking every last bit of life energy from her.

"It was an interesting five years, Deborah," he said, raising his glass in a toast. "I can't say you were a worthy opponent. But for a while there, the sex was great."

And it had been, which should have clued her to what he really was.

Energy between a Primal and a Libertas in sex could be almost explosive, since they fed back and forth off each other, sometimes cycling energy up into mind-blowing events.

They had had a few such events right before and right after they were married, but she considered them only the passion of their newlywed moments.

And she had always considered him nothing more than a cow.

He had known better.

And just as with every time he married a Primal, he had hoped she would love him enough to not turn him into a cow.

But in thousands of years of marriages now, that had never happened.

But someday he would find the Primal of his dreams. And she would not turn him into a cow, not want to turn him into a cow, and he would not end up killing her for her greed.

A fella could only hope.

Across from him, the dust that had been Deborah just slowly settled onto the chair and on the floor.

Every bit of life energy she had was now his.

He finished his drink and went to get the vacuum cleaner.

And to see who had ended up winning that last baseball game.

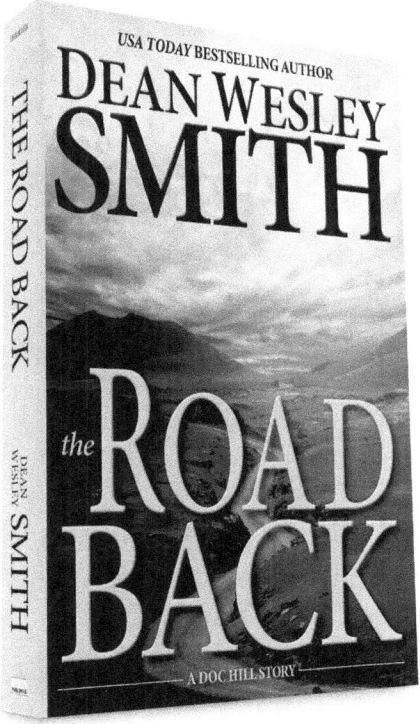

USA Today Bestselling Writer

DEAN WESLEY SMITH

She Hid Her Money
And So Much More

THE CASE OF
THE LOST TREASURE

A Pilgrim Hugh Incident

Hired by heirs to find two million in treasure hidden in a completely empty house, Pilgrim Hugh finds himself stuck.

The house sparkles and no stick of furniture remains.

Original house plans show clearly that no room hid behind any walls. And millions of dollars in cash takes up a bunch of room. But where?

A puzzle mystery that stumps for a short time even the great Pilgrim Hugh.

THE CASE OF
THE LOST TREASURE
A Pilgrim Hugh Incident

ONE

PILGRIM HUGH TRIED to gather his thoughts as he stared out the front window of the four-bedroom home in the northwest section of Portland. The early fall day outside was warm and the lush green of the oak trees that lined the quiet street had not even hinted at turning to fall colors.

The home still had its air-conditioning set at a comfortable seventy degrees, even though no one lived in the home. Every stick of furniture had been removed from the house two months before when Mary Ellen Ryan died at eighty-six.

The air smelled of a lemon-scented cleaner and the old hardwood floors shone under a fresh polish. The walls had been freshly painted a soft, eggshell and the walnut baseboards and door trims had also been polished.

The place sparkled, ready to be shown to a new buyer as soon as he solved this case.

And Pilgrim had no doubt the house would sell quickly. It was in a wonderful neighborhood on a large lot with flowers and large trees. The house had been built in the early 1920s and clearly maintained along the way, sporting a newly remodeled kitchen and bathroom.

Pilgrim wore jeans, tennis shoes, and a light blue dress shirt with his sleeves rolled up. Over the last hour and ten minutes he had become very, very familiar with the home as he looked at every wall and every board in the floors.

Somewhere in this home was a treasure trove of over a million dollars in cash, maybe more. He had been hired to find it by the two sons of the woman who had lived here.

A challenging case to say the least. And he loved challenging cases. It was what he lived for, actually.

He had ended up a private detective through a series of strange events. First, three years of law school and a failed first marriage while working for a corporate law firm had convinced him he wasn't a normal lawyer.

Or a decent standard husband either. In fact, he sucked at both.

Then his grandmother had died and left him more money than he could imagine, which sent him on a year of traveling and drinking, which eventually got very, very boring.

On a lark, a few weeks after he stopped drinking to excess, he went back to school to become a private detective. After he hung out his shingle, he learned that being a private eye wasn't what the detective novels described. It was all computer work and long boring hours of nothingness trying to watch someone.

At that point, he had finally caught a simple clue that his problem was he bored easily. He needed some excitement and challenges in his life.

So with some of his grandmother's money, he set up Hugh and Associates, a combination law firm and private investigative firm. Then he had hired a couple great associates who took all the boring cases and made the firm lots of money and they hired even more associates that he had no desire to meet who also made him lots and lots of money.

 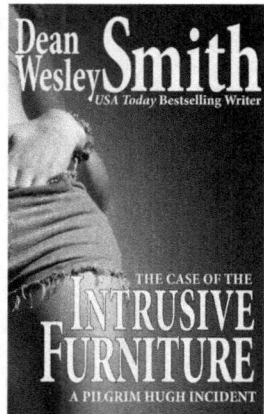 

Three Pilgrim Hugh Incidents
Available at your favorite booksellers.

And he also discovered he was pretty good at real estate investment, so his money made even more money and an entire floor in his office building handled his investments in commercial and apartment complex real estate.

He had then offered for free his investigative state-of-the-art services to surrounding police forces. As it turned out, they liked free and he had helped solved some really interesting cases.

Seldom boring.

And finding this money was far from boring as well, although not brought to him by a police force.

Benson and Brad Ryan had hired him to find their mother's treasure trove, as they called it. They were twin sons of Mary Ellen Ryan who had lived in this house for forty years before dying from a stroke. She had told them about the money, that it was hidden here in the house, and that when she was gone they needed to find it.

So the two twins were stuck. They couldn't even begin to probate their mother's estate until they knew about all the assets. And a million or more in cash were a lot of assets.

When Pilgrim had talked to them about the case, sitting in his office in his building, he had asked a very simple question. "How did your mother manage to get that much cash?"

They had both laughed.

"She was the child of Depression parents," Brad had explained. "She had been left wealthy by her father, their grandfather, when he died when they were in college thirty years earlier."

Benson nodded. "Mom and Dad bought the house she was in after we were out of college. She would take five thousand dollars out of her bank account in cash every week, for miscellaneous expenses, as she called them."

"She would maybe spend a few hundred of the money," Brad said, "and the rest would vanish into what she called her fund that she had set aside in case the banks closed. She did that for years and years."

"She made sure to tell us that there was at least a million dollars or more hidden in her house," Benson said.

"But she never once told us where it was," Brad said.

Pilgrim stared at the beautiful lawn and the street shaded by tall trees. This really was a very private neighborhood and a very nice home.

Pilgrim turned around and put his back to the big window to once again stare into the empty house.

It was here. He knew that. And in a place that an elderly Mary Ellen Ryan could access easily every week, since her husband had been dead for the last thirty years.

The puzzle was where.

Why was it taking him so long to figure it out?

TWO

PILGRIM'S ASSISTANT DONNA came through the front door holding a folder of paper. Today, as she did most days in the summer, Donna wore skintight white shorts, a halter-top, and tennis shoes. She had short brown hair and wide brown eyes and a smile that could blind a room.

She kept herself in perfect shape with more exercise every day than Pilgrim could imagine any human doing.

Not only was Donna stunningly good-looking, but she was also an expert in high-speed driving, guns, and computers. It was her computer skills that Pilgrim treasured the most. She could find information that normal computer experts would never find.

And do it fast.

Donna, like Pilgrim, hated to be bored.

"So how goes The Case of the Lost Treasure?" Donna asked, handing Pilgrim the file.

Donna loved to name each of their cases, which she said later helped make it easier for them to remember and for her to file, even though she did no real filing. She had an assistant to do that sort of thing.

"We are still standing here," Pilgrim said. "After one hour and thirteen minutes."

"So not well," Donna said.

"This is a puzzle, I must admit," Pilgrim said.

He sat down on the polished wood floor and started to spread out the sheets of paper from the file. Donna had somehow managed to find original plans for the house and printed them in their high-tech limo that served as their office. She had also pulled all the plans and permits for any remodeling that had been done on record for this home.

Pilgrim had a hunch that this treasure trove hiding place had not been a sanctioned remodel.

Donna walked through the place while he worked at the paper. There was a modern kitchen redone twenty years before and he had the permits and plans for that, as well as the remodeling of the one bathroom done at the same time.

Her sons had told Pilgrim she had gone to Europe during the two months of the remodeling.

The original plans showed the same layout that was in the house now. No missing spaces at all. And considering that most of the walls of this house were plaster and lathe, that didn't surprise him. Changing those walls around would be a horrid pain and a very dirty and time-consuming process.

So the money was not in a secret room or a fake back of a large closet or anything like that.

There were no other records of any construction at all on the home.

None.

Donna came back into the living room area as he was gathering up the papers.

"This place is lovely," she said. "Real old charm, great neighborhood. Quiet."

"Maybe you should buy it," Pilgrim said.

Donna laughed and shook her head. "Not my style."

She took the folder he handed her as he stood.

"No luck?" she asked.

"The original construction plan matches the home plan as it sits," he said. "Right down to the coal chute into the small basement area where the old coal burning furnace used to be."

Suddenly, the thought of going downstairs gave Pilgrim an idea. He remembered that the twins had said something about their mother enjoying her wine. They called it her only vice. Benson had said that she called it her hobby.

"Would you call the twins and ask them about the wine their mother drank? Where it was stored in the kitchen?"

Donna frowned and nodded while Pilgrim went to the door just off the kitchen that led down into the small basement space. He had inspected that small base-ment very carefully twice already. It was a logical place for a stash of money, but there was no sign it was there.

But the space he had missed was the transition into the basement and the wine was the key to all of this.

He clicked on the light and started down the wood steps. He could imagine Mary Ellen holding the solid wood hand-rail as she went down. Although there was little reason to ever go into the basement.

The stairs went down ten steps to a wide landing and then turned to the left and went another four steps into the base-ment room, even though there was more than enough room for the steps to go on straight.

He had a hunch they originally had gone straight and then had been replaced with this newer staircase.

Pilgrim stood on the landing staring at the basement room for a moment where the old coal burner had sat before being replaced by a much smaller gas furnace.

Then he turned completely around, his back to the basement, and stared at the wood wall that bordered the inside of the stairs.

He saw nothing.

No scrape on the landing floor where a door might have swung open, no sign at all that the wood had a seam or hinges or anything.

He studied the wall for a moment, then climbed back up two steps and stopped and turned around again to face the landing.

The wine was the key. The room was behind that wall. But how to get into it yet needed to be puzzled out.

At the top of the stairs Donna appeared, looking like a mostly naked angel glowing from the hall light behind her.

"Benson said she always had a really nice, often expensive bottle of wine," Donna said. "They just assumed she bought them regularly and stored them in the kitchen somewhere."

Pilgrim nodded. Mary Ellen not only had a safe room for her money, but more than likely had amassed a large wine collection.

Pilgrim glanced up at the glowing Donna. She looked like a photo shoot model the way the lights played on her as she stood silhouetted in the doorway.

And beside her was the light switch to the basement. Only it had four switches on it and only the first switch worked.

Of course.

"Call him back and have him and his brother come over as quickly as possible. I have found the hidden room, but do not want to open it without them being here."

"You found it?" Donna asked as Pilgrim came back up the stairs.

"I did," he said, "and I'm annoyed at myself for not finding it sooner. It took me one hour and twenty-seven minutes to solve this."

Donna just stared at him, shook her head, and then turned to make the phone call.

Maybe he was slipping a little.

Later he would need to think through his process again on this over a good glass of wine.

THREE

WHEN THE TWO brothers came into the home, Pilgrim was drinking from a water bottle and leaning against the counter near the sink.

He had had Donna go to the limo to get him a bottle of water and to also research where Mary Ellen had bought her wine and how much she had bought.

It turned out, she had been a major customer of three different wine shops in town, often buying wine by the case and having it delivered. And she loved vintage wines.

Expensive vintage wines.

Pilgrim looked at some of her purchases and felt a little twist of envy. Mary Ellen had purchased wines he had only hoped to find a bottle of some day.

Both brothers came into the kitchen followed by Donna. Both were in almost matching dark blue business suits and clearly had come quickly from their offices. Pilgrim knew that both worked in corporate jobs in the downtown area close to this section of town and both were very well off. They actually didn't need their mother's money. They just wanted to get the estate taxes done and for the estate to close.

"That was surprisingly fast," Brad said.

"Very fast," Benson said. "We looked for two months for the hidden money room and you found it in an hour."

Donna raised an eyebrow and gave Pilgrim a smile.

"An hour and twenty-seven minutes," Pilgrim said.

The two brothers both laughed.

"There will be more than money in the room," Pilgrim said. "So prepare yourself for that."

"Have you opened it?" Brad asked.

"I have not," Pilgrim said. "But your mother was a major wine collector."

"She was?" Benson asked.

"She and dad used to enjoy going to vineyards," Brad said. "But I never knew she collected."

Pilgrim nodded. "She had, it seems, very good taste in her collection as well. So where she stashed the money was also where she kept her wine safe and dark and at the right temperature."

Both brothers looked at each other, clearly feeling stunned.

"So head on down to the basement," Pilgrim said, "and we all will see this mysterious room."

"We checked that basement a hundred times," Brad said, shaking his head.

"The room is very well hidden," Pilgrim said.

Brad and Benson went down the stairs and into the basement, followed by Donna.

Pilgrim stayed at the top of the stairs until they were turned around and looking back up at him.

"What day and month was your mother's birthday?"

"April 14th," Benson said.

Pilgrim shook his head. That won't work.

"Your birthday?"

"October 1st," Brad said.

Pilgrim smiled. "Your mother was very smart."

Pilgrim looked at the four light switches at the top of the stairs. They just looked to be normal. The first one was already up, since the lights below were on. He left the second one down. Then he left the third switch down as well and flipped up the fourth switch.

There was a good seven-second delay, as he had expected so no one accidently would hit the combination by just flipping switches randomly. Then the entire landing wall swung inward with almost no sound and lights came up in the room beyond.

"Holy shit," Brad said.

"How did you open that?" Benson asked as Pilgrim came down the stairs and the two twins started up from the basement.

"The four light switches at the top of the stairs. Your birthday. 1001. October 1st. First switch up, two down, last switch up."

"How the hell did you figure that out?" Benson asked, shaking his head.

"This is what I do," Pilgrim said.

Then he let the two brothers lead the four steps down into the large wine cellar. He and Donna followed.

Pilgrim had to admit, the sight was impressive. And at a glance he could tell there were some of the best wines from around the world stored here. He would love to have this wine collection in his wine room in his penthouse apartment.

He had far overbuilt his wine room when he took the penthouse, and had had little luck in filling it with the types of wines he hoped to find. This collection would go a long ways to filling that room.

The hidden room was at a perfect temperature to store wine in a dark and cool place. Mary Ellen had done this right in every detail. Of that, Pilgrim had no doubt.

"There has to be a couple thousand bottles of wine down here," Brad said, his voice almost a whisper as if normal speech might hurt the wine.

Pilgrim pointed to the wall on the left. It was covered with metal cabinets. "Might want to check those out."

Both Brad and Benson walked over to different metal cabinets and opened them. As Mary Ellen had told them, she had a stash of money, all hundreds, banded in five thousand dollar stacks.

There were ten double-door cabinets along the wall and the brothers opened them all, finding them all full of nothing but money.

By Pilgrim's rough estimate, that was far, far more than a million dollars.

Both brothers just looked shocked.

They turned to him, smiles looking like they might twist their faces out of shape.

"How can we ever thank you?" Brad said. "We never would have found this and I doubt anyone else would have either."

"I have a suggestion toward the thanking discussion," Pilgrim said.

"And what might that be?" Brad asked, glancing back at the stacks of money.

"Get this wine appraised by an expert for the estate," Pilgrim said, "and then sell it to me at a reasonable price."

"You have room for all this?" Benson asked, glancing around at the thousands of bottles of top wines his mother had collected.

"I do," Pilgrim said. "I am a collector of fine wines as your mother was and owning this collection would be a wonderful way to remember this case."

Benson glanced at his brother who nodded.

"I think we can do that just fine," Benson said.

"Considering that neither of us drink wine," Brad said, laughing, "I am sure mother would want us to sell her collection to someone who would appreciate it."

Pilgrim looked around at all the racks of perfectly stored expensive vintage wine. It was almost enough to get his mouth watering.

"She would find no one who would appreciate it more," Pilgrim said.

And that might have been the biggest understatement he had ever uttered.

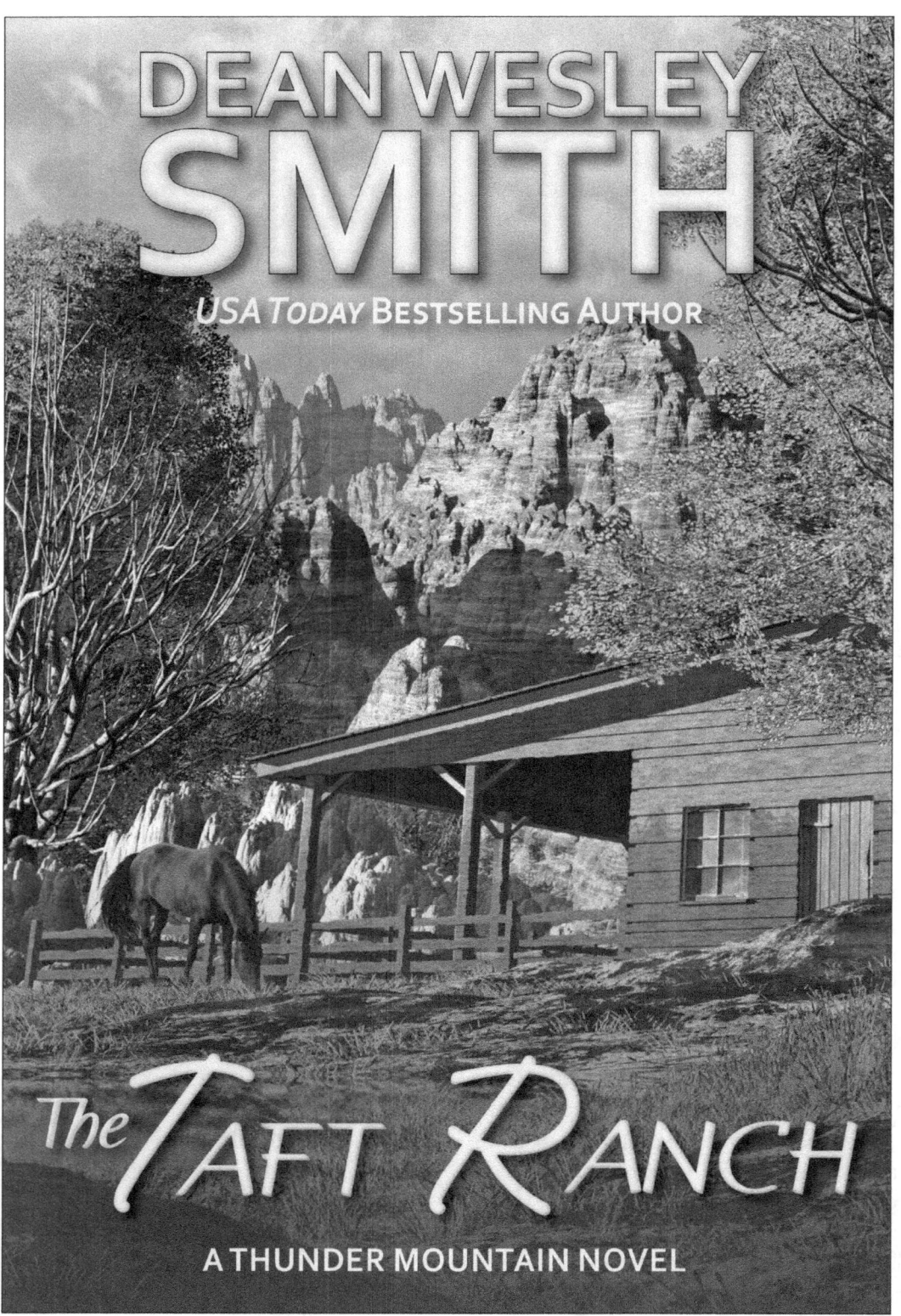

DEAN WESLEY
SMITH

USA Today Bestselling Author

The Taft Ranch

A THUNDER MOUNTAIN NOVEL

Duster Kendal knows something must be wrong when a tree blocks the road to the Taft Ranch. Turns out Lee Taft failed to return from his last trip into the past.

Duster fears the worst, that time kicked Lee into a distant and inhospitable future with no hope of return. And no hope of rescue.

A story of survival through centuries of time.

USA Today *bestselling writer Dean Wesley Smith takes readers once again into his fan favorite Thunder Mountain time travel series, but this time into the distant future instead of the near past.*

THE TAFT RANCH
A Thunder Mountain Novel

For Kris

PART ONE
Missing

ONE

August 7th, 2018
Central, Idaho

THE ROAD WAS blocked, but it shouldn't have been.

Duster Kendal climbed out of his white Cadillac SUV and stared at the narrow-tracked road that wound up a steep valley between rocks and pine trees.

A tree was down across the road now, and had clearly fallen at least a few weeks back.

No sign at all that anyone had tried to clear the tree or even parked in front of it and walked around it.

Lee Taft lived in a wonderful ranch up that road. When Lee got back from the past each time, he always came in here to work and be away from the world and get lost in his math, as he liked to say.

But now the road was blocked. Duster had driven that narrow road a hundred times and ridden on horse up it even more.

Lee, if he was here, would not have allowed that road to be blocked for more than a day.

The air around Duster was warm, even at eleven in the morning, and a light breeze brought him the scent of hot pine and sagebrush.

Duster had left his usual long oilcloth coat and cowboy hat in the back seat of the car and wore only jeans, a thin white dress shirt, and cowboy boots. But if it got much warmer, he would put on both the coat and the hat. It was amazing how that long oil-cloth coat kept him cooler, especially combined with the wide cowboy hat that kept the mountain sun off his face.

He stared around at the high rock-covered mountains that towered above the narrow valley, turning slowly to take it all in.

The road he had come into the area on was a single-lane dirt and gravel road which headed down a valley toward the two old Idaho mining towns of Big Creek and Edwardsburg, Idaho. He was still about twenty minutes from their locations.

Duster had stayed last night up at the Monumental Summit lodge, which looked close to this spot on a map, but it had still taken him almost two hours after a late breakfast to go down the mountain to the small town of Yellow Pine and then

turn on the gravel Big Creek road to get to where he was now.

He knew he was in the right location. This was Lee's road.

The Taft Ranch was in a wide area of the valley a mile up the narrow canyon. The ranch house itself Duster had helped build numbers of times back in 1890 and he loved the place.

Lee Taft, one of the best mathematicians to come along, and a good friend, built and lived at the ranch, both when he was back in history and in the present time.

And in all the times Lee was a regular at the Monumental Summit Lodge during the summer months. It was his absence from his regular visits to the Lodge this summer that had worried Dawn Edwards, another historian who worked and partially owned the lodge, and she had mentioned it to Duster who said he would go check on Lee.

Duster had figured Lee had gotten busy on some research and hadn't allowed himself time away from the ranch.

But the tree down meant that Lee was either sick up at the ranch or had never returned to the ranch for some reason.

Duster turned and went back to the car, taking out the satellite phone he kept in the car when in the Idaho central mountains. Regular cell service up here was just a laughing matter.

He called Dawn at the lodge. When she answered, he said, "There is a tree blocking the road going into Lee's ranch. He is either really sick or he clearly hasn't been here since he left to go into the past."

"What?" Dawn asked.

"It feels as if something has gone wrong, very wrong. I'm going to hike into the ranch house site and see if Lee is there. But first I want you to get a hold of Bonnie and also Brice and Dixie and Director Parks. I want all four of them to go together into the crystal cavern Lee was using to travel back into time. I'll wait here for what they find before heading up the valley toward Lee's place."

Dawn was silent for a moment, then said, "I'll be back with you quickly."

Duster closed the car door and turned on the air-conditioning. He had a horrid feeling about what they might find. But he didn't want to think about it until they actually went into the crystal room under the Institute in Boise.

It was those crystals that allowed them all to travel into other timelines and effectively the past.

He just sat staring down the road toward Edwardsburg for over ten minutes until his phone rang.

It was his wife, Bonnie.

She didn't even say hello.

"One of the machines was still hooked up to a crystal and had been now for at least a month. Maybe longer. The crystal record has Lee's name on it."

Travel into the past only took two minutes and fifteen seconds of present time. No exception. No crystal could be hooked up for longer than that time.

At least until now.

"When was it set for?" Duster asked.

"May 2nd, 1955," Bonnie said.

It was exactly what Duster had feared when he saw the blocked road going into Lee's ranch.

"We unhooked the crystal," Bonnie said. "And marked it."

"No Lee, I assume."

"No Lee," she said. "Nothing happened at all."

He took a deep breath and nodded to himself. Lee was no longer in that timeline.

"All four of you get ready to fly into the lodge for an early dinner tonight. I'm going to hike up to the location of Lee's home and see what I can see. I'll call you from there."

"Okay," Bonnie said. "Be cautious."

"Thanks," he said. "I will."

With that he climbed out of the SUV, put on his cowboy hat and long duster coat, and then with a bottle of water in each pocket and the satellite phone in another, he headed into the brush around the fallen tree and up the narrow canyon, following the old road he remembered.

His stomach twisted for the entire hike, worried about what he might find.

And he honestly had no idea what that might be.

And he had no idea what might have caused Lee to not return to the present in the normal two-minute time.

But he had a hunch.

And that hunch scared him more than he wanted to think about.

TWO

September 14th, 1980
Central, Idaho

DR. LEE TAFT loved his ranch.

He loved everything about it, from the towering rock peaks behind it to the beauty of the valley spread out below it. He loved the rustic, log-hewn barn that was dug into the side of one hill. That was where he kept his two horses and all the feed they would need.

His ranch house was partially dug into the hill as well just above the barn and protected by large, water-smoothed rocks. It was also made of thick logs and thick, hand-cut wooden shingles that kept the house cool in the summer and warm in the long winters.

He had cut every log himself, every shingle, every post and beam. Duster had helped a few times, but most of the times Lee had done it all himself.

And got the logs and beams into place himself. At six-one, Lee had gained his strength and love of the outdoors from his father who had taught Lee from a little child to camp and work hard, both physically and with his brain.

Lee loved the large living room in his ranch home with two comfortable cloth couches, a large reading chair, and a massive stone fireplace against the far wall, now blackened from so many years of daily fires. Thick quilts he had made himself were always tossed haphazardly over the backs of the chairs or two couches.

The kitchen sat off to the left of the living room, with the large wood dining table separating the two. He usually kept that table covered with notebooks full of his calculations.

He had built the ranch in the remote Idaho central wilderness in the summer of 1890, the first time to do research on the mathematical impact of time-traveler events on timelines. The remote location and doing the work himself was his way of trying not to impact the very thing he was studying.

He was thirty-two when he built the ranch and had left it in 1920 when he was seventy-two. He had put everything into his secret back room and sealed it against any access.

Then he became thirty-two again in 2018 and reset the same timeline crystal and came back again in 1925, pretending

to be his own grandson who had inherited the ranch. He stayed at the ranch until 1950 when he was fifty-seven. Then he left, went back to 2018 and became 32 again and came back again in 1955, pretending to be his own son.

He didn't leave the ranch again in 1980, one hundred years after he had built it.

He loved that pattern so much, he kept repeating it, timeline by timeline. And when he got back to the future, he always fixed the place up again.

So far he had built the ranch in 1890 thirty-six times and couldn't imagine tiring of doing it again.

He had studied thirty-six timelines and patterns were starting to emerge as to how timeline travelers like him caused ripples over many timelines. His math was getting more and more complicated with each lifetime in the past.

Usually between each leg of the trip he spent time in 2018, working with other mathematicians who knew about timeline travel, and meeting with Bonnie and Duster Kendal about his work since they were two of the most brilliant minds in all of mathematics.

All of them were excited about his work and wanted him to keep going. Lee needed no such encouragement. He was excited as well.

He hated being away from the seclusion of the ranch and the remoteness of the past longer than that. The seclusion allowed him to really think clearly and the physical work of first building the ranch and then keeping the ranch in shape helped keep him healthy and feeling young.

The next time back he planned on bringing back to the secret room in the back of the ranch a new, smaller, far more powerful computer system from 2118, run from solar power. The secret room buried in the hill behind his ranch house was protected from any intruders with alarms and explosives that would destroy everything unless he disarmed it.

Bonnie and Duster hated taking anything from the future back into the past, but had given Lee special permission since his work on timelines and the influence of future travelers was making such great progress.

The new computer would allow him to crunch the massive numbers of equations he needed to work through.

The ranch was so isolated that he couldn't tell much difference from the 1890s time and the 1980s time. Just how he got his regular supplies changed as the years went by.

Duster often stopped by in different time frames. Lee considered Duster one of his only friends and their conversations on historical events and mathematics were always fascinating and often led to Lee working along a different line of research.

But when it came right down to it, he loved being alone to do his writing and his research. And in living now for hundreds of years of time, it had never crossed his mind to be lonely or even wish for companionship.

His work was his companionship, his ranch his true love.

THREE

May 3rd, 1986
Boise, Idaho

DR. JOAN FAILOR was deep in thought on an important chapter in her new book on coma states when the phone on her desk rang.

She felt like she had suddenly been returned from a great distance to her office and slapped at the same time.

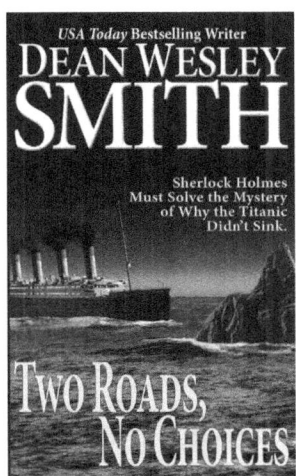
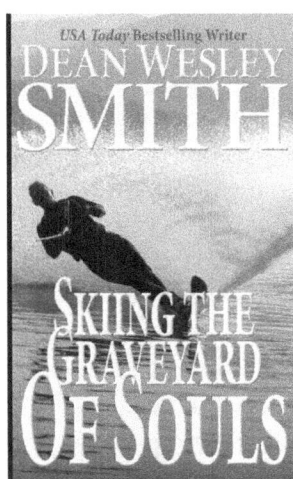

Around her the plush furnishings of the private office seemed to almost tilt, then settle as the adrenalin surge of the surprise passed and was replaced by annoyance at the interruption. Steph, her secretary, knew better than to bother her.

Joan had been sitting in her favorite reading chair. Behind her the window was letting in orange light from a promising warm spring day.

Her office had a large leather couch against one wall and her reading chair sat in front of the window that looked out over the tree-filled park that was part of the grounds of her building. Her large mahogany desk dominated the room and at the moment was covered with fewer papers than normal.

The wall behind her desk was built-in mahogany bookcases filled with books, many of them she had written or contributed articles to. At thirty-five, she was already one of the most respected authorities on the brain and on deep coma sleep in the nation.

The phone rang again and she laid aside her pad filled with notes and stood, getting to the phone on the corner of her desk before it rang again.

"I was not to be disturbed."

"I'm sorry, doctor," Steph said. "But I was convinced you would want to know he was awake."

Steph was not only Joan's secretary, but she was also Joan's best friend. In the office and around the patients, Steph was all business. But away from the office the two of them had been known to knock down a few cocktails in their time.

Joan stood five-ten, kept her blonde hair cut short and styled, and seldom went anywhere in the building without her white smock to show authority. She owned the place, after all. Under the smock she always had on jeans, usually a light silk blouse, and comfortable shoes.

Steph always dressed the part of an expensive secretary. She kept her long blonde hair pulled back and wielded more power around the building that Joan did at times. She had master's degrees in both business and office management and an MBA. No one crossed Steph.

Joan couldn't imagine doing this job without Steph at her side. They had been friends since college.

"Who's awake?" Joan said, trying to get herself focused and out of the work she had just been doing.

"Lee Taft," Steph said.

Joan just couldn't accept what Steph was saying. That wasn't possible.

"What do you mean he's awake?" Joan asked, trying to get her balance. "Why the hell would he wake up suddenly now?"

"He just blinked, woke up and asked for a drink of water," Steph said.

"Not possible," Joan said, hanging up on Steph and heading out the door at a fast run. "He shouldn't even be able to talk for days."

Steph joined her as they both left the office suite together, heading for the elevator to go down four floors in the big building where Lee Taft had been in a coma for the past six years.

There were over fifty patients in this building in different states of comas.

Lee Taft had been a man in his late fifties when he was bucked off a horse just outside of Cascade, Idaho, and hit his head and severed part of his spinal cord. That back injury had paralyzed him from the waist down. How he had survived that accident was beyond Joan, but he had.

She had first met him after he was stabilized. He was in a deep coma, but his brain clearly had activity and seemed to be functioning fine. Only they couldn't wake him up.

After ten weeks in the hospital, she had had him transferred to her building for long-term care, since he had no family or even friends anyone could find. It seemed he had lived alone on a family ranch in the central wilderness area for twenty-five years.

As his medical guardian, she had had the ranch put in a trust for when he woke up, if he ever woke up. And he had become one of her most important cases of study.

A healthy man, a mostly healthy body, a brain injury that kept him in a coma, even though it seemed that brain activity didn't slow down in the slightest. And the actual injury to the brain had healed.

At times she had people reading to him and everyone just called him Lee when around him, treating him with respect. Over the years his hair had turned even grayer and more lines had formed on his face, but they had managed with exercise to keep his muscles very healthy. All but his legs.

It seemed to Joan to take an eternity to get down to the second floor and off the elevator. Joan was almost shaking and Steph seemed to be bouncing. Steph had really come to like Lee, even though he had been in a coma. She looked at him as a grandfather she had never had.

Actually, everyone on the staff liked Lee, even though he had never said a word or even blinked an eye.

Joan made it to the familiar room that she had visited hundreds of times over the last six years. They had decorated Lee's private room in western decorations, from pictures of horses to men in cowboy hats. The furniture even had a wood and cloth décor more suited for a farmhouse than a long-term care facility.

The machines monitoring his vital signs were tucked away in a cabinet that was now open. Joan glanced at the machine as she entered. It was clear Lee's heart and breathing were completely normal for an awake person.

This room was part of what Joan did for those in her care. She tried to put them in surroundings that they might feel comfortable with if they ever woke up. It also made the patients feel more human to the staff working around and on them.

As she got closer to the bed she was startled by the intense brown eyes of Lee Taft looking up at her. He seemed to have a depth and intelligence that now radiated from his eyes.

Steph stopped in the doorway and just stared

Craig, one of the nurses and Steph's most recent love interest, stood beside Lee's bed. Joan could see why Steph was interested in the guy. He was a hunk, that was for sure.

"We dressed Lee for your visit," Craig said. "He asked to at least be in a shirt and pants.

She nodded and Craig moved over to the door beside Steph.

"I'm Dr. Joan Failor," Joan said, moving up and smiling at Lee. He was laying there in one of his own flannel shirts and jeans, a wide buckle at his waist and socks on his feet. They had kept his original clothes cleaned and ready for him. Luckily they had.

For some reason, she felt instantly attracted to him, far more than a simple favorite patient attraction.

He stared at her as well for a moment, then shook his head and said, "Lee Taft. Call me Lee. It's nice to meet you, Doctor."

She laughed. "It's really nice to meet you as well, Lee."

"So, where am I," Lee asked. "And how come I can't feel my legs?"

"It seems you fell off a horse," Joan said, deciding that since he was so clearly awake now, he could handle some of the truth. Often they kept some of what had happened from those coming out of a coma because loved ones had died in the same event.

But Lee had been alone and had no family that they had ever found.

Lee actually laughed at that, the sound raspy. He shook his head. "Only fell off twice in all the years."

"You broke part of your back and were in a coma from a head injury," Joan said. "Which is why you are here in my building. We are not sure why you picked this moment to suddenly awake."

"Coma?" Lee asked, now suddenly seeming slightly worried. He wasn't worried that he had broken his back and couldn't feel his legs. He was worried that he had been asleep.

"I'm afraid so," Joan said. "We weren't certain that you would ever wake up, even though your brain scans showed complete activity. As I said, we're not sure why you suddenly did now, but are very glad you did."

Lee suddenly looked a little panicked. "How long was I in the coma?"

Joan usually hated to tell anyone the number at first, but Lee was clearly back and in full control of his mind.

"About six years," Joan said.

Now the calm, deep, intelligent eyes of Lee Taft went into complete panic.

"The date? What's today's date?"

Joan looked puzzled and glanced around at Steph and Craig who were also looking puzzled. Both of them were taking notes, which is what Joan needed.

She turned back to Lee. "May 3rd, 1986."

Full panic hit Lee's face. He suddenly looked as if he was being chased by more creatures from the worst movie ever seen.

"Lee, what's wrong?" Joan asked. "What happened, what did you miss?"

Lee shook his head from side-to-side, the panic not leaving his face.

He just kept muttering, "This can't be happening. This can't be happening."

"Can you tell me what is happening?" Joan asked, easing closer to Lee and trying to comfort him. She had seen many patients come out of comas over the years, and often have a reaction about how much time they have lost. But nothing like this.

"I need to get to the Historical Research Institute," he said. "Down on Warm Springs Ave. As soon as possible."

"Why?" Joan asked.

"Because today's my birthday," Lee said.

As if that would explain everything, but to Joan it explained nothing. And what a historical research institute had to do with anything she had no idea.

"Well," Joan said, trying to smile. "Happy birthday."

"It won't be if I can't get to the institute before ten-fifteen in the morning."

Joan glanced at her watch. "I'm afraid that won't be possible. It's already ten-fourteen."

Lee grabbed both her arms, the panic clear in his eyes. His grip was amazingly tight for a man who had been in a coma for so long. Clearly the medical exercises they had continued to do with him over the years had kept his muscles working fine.

"Why are you so panicked?" Joan asked. "You are here. It's safe."

"Because today is my birthday," Lee said, not letting go of her arms. "I can't be here. Time won't let me be here."

And as he said that, Joan found herself sitting in the dirt with Lee still holding onto her arms.

His room was gone.

Steph and Craig were gone.

Her building was gone.

Everything was gone.

Only thing around them was a massive and magnificent crystal cavern, shaped like a huge dome with a flat dirt floor. Every inch of the walls were covered in glowing pink crystals that looked like a form of quartz.

She blinked. This wasn't possible.

Not possible.

"Oh, no," Lee said, letting go of her arms and moving away from her. "Oh, no, what have I done? I didn't mean to bring you with me. I didn't. I am so sorry."

"Where are we?" Joan asked, her voice hoarse.

"Oh, no, what have I done," he repeated. "I am so, so sorry."

She looked around, trying to make any sense of what she was seeing. Clearly, it was all a hallucination. It had to be.

"Lee," she said, trying to keep the panic from her voice. "Where are we?"

"We're in the Nexus," Lee said. "I've never been here before, but I know what Duster has described and this is the Nexus."

As she watched, Lee stood and looked around like a kid staring at tall buildings in a city for the first time.

Joan pushed herself to her feet.

"How can you stand up?" Joan asked, staring at Lee.

And then she staggered back, feeling even more of a shock as he turned to face her.

He was her age.

The gray hair was gone, the lines in his face were gone.

He was handsome and young, with a full head of brown hair.

She felt the cavern start to spin around her and she decided at that moment it was just better to sit back down.

Lee caught her in strong, young hands before she fell in her attempt to sit.

FOUR

Time: Unknown
Nexus

LEE EASED THE beautiful doctor down to the flat dirt floor of the large cavern, then sat down beside her.

Around them the cavern felt like they were sitting on the fifty-yard line of a major football stadium. Actually, this cavern could take just about every major football stadium and have room left over.

Pink quartz-like crystals covered every inch of the massive cavern, glowing with enough light to make the cavern seem like it was almost bathed in defused sunlight.

Every crystal represented a timeline. This was what he had been studying for hundreds of years. And Duster had described the Nexus many times in their conversations and had even offered to bring Lee to see the little part closest to the surface, but they had never gotten around to it.

He wanted to touch the doctor's arm, to try to calm her, but decided it was better to just let her have a moment. He had been around so few women over all the years, he actually had no idea what to do to help her.

"So what happened?" Dr. Failor asked finally after about thirty seconds. Her voice was shaking.

Interestingly, her reaction was calming Lee's panic. He could feel his brain starting to work to solve this problem, if there was a solution.

"By holding onto you in my panic," Lee said, "I accidently brought you with me. I am so, so sorry, Doctor Failor."

"Call me Joan," she said.

He nodded and said nothing.

"You knew this might happen?" Joan asked.

"I didn't know what would happen, honestly," Lee said, shaking his head. "That's why I was so panicked. I couldn't be there on my birthday."

"As if this isn't bad enough," Joan said, waving her arms around her at the fantastic beauty of the massive chamber, "you are still not making one bit of sense."

Lee nodded. "I suppose you will believe me if I tell you the truth, with all this?"

He indicated the cavern.

"Any kind of explanation would be helpful at this point," Joan said. "But please, yes the truth."

Lee could tell she was getting angry and he didn't need her angry. Actually, if they had any hope of getting out of this alive, he needed her working with him.

But he doubted they would get out of this alive.

"I was born on May 3rd, 1986, in Boise, Idaho," Lee said. "When I said it was my birthday, I meant it was my real birthday. More than likely the process of my starting to be born was what brought me out of the coma after all the years."

Joan looked at him, opened her mouth, then shut it, shaking her head.

"I am a mathematician," Lee said, "and I had traveled into a different timeline through crystals like all these. There are crystals like these taken from a cavern like this under the Historical Research Institute in Boise. I left the institute in

2018 and traveled back to 1955. I planned on returning to 2018 in 1980, but the accident stopped that, it seemed."

Joan just stared at him, not saying anything.

He pushed on. "All of these crystals represent a different timeline. Every time anyone makes a decision or when there is more than one outcome to something, two timelines are formed, one for each outcome."

"There would be an infinite number of timelines," Joan said, her voice flat.

Lee was very glad she understood that. In the long run, that would help a lot.

"There are," Lee said. "These crystals represent just the place where time and energy and matter meet. These caverns are infinite."

"Oh," was all she said.

Lee could see the panic in her face again starting to build.

"One major rule of timelines is that you can't be in the timeline when you were originally alive in it."

"Thus the importance of your birthday?" she asked, taking some deep breaths.

Lee nodded. "If you die in another timeline, you just go back to when you started. So if the horse accident would have killed me, I would have ended up back in 2018 just fine, no worse for wear. In essence, what happens in another timeline doesn't affect you in your original timeline, other than you lose a few minutes of life."

"That's why you look to be thirty now?" Joan asked.

"I'm thirty-two," Lee said, then he looked around. "At least I was when I left 2018."

"So how did we end up here?"

"Two of me couldn't be alive in the same timeline," Lee said. "So the timeline spit this me, the interloper from another timeline, out. Because I was panicked and holding onto you, I brought you with me. Again I am so sorry."

"You don't seem that surprised you are here," Joan said.

"Being spit out of a timeline and into the Nexus is one of the theories. I'm afraid we are the first to test that theory."

"Oh, great," she said.

He stood and offered her his hand. "We need to get moving."

"To where?" she asked. "Didn't you say these caverns are infinite?"

"I did," Lee said. "But Duster and I have theorized that time will spit an interloper out at the first place that person didn't exist. So I'm guessing that in these crystals in this room, I don't exist."

Joan looked around at the huge chamber, and the massive area where it joined another chamber on one side and the same sized archway on the other, making them look like linked bubbles.

"How do you know which way to go?"

"We go uphill," Lee said. "Where Duster found the cavern with the timelines closest to our world was near the surface."

They started off walking at a fast pace. It was clear to Lee they were going uphill. But it was also clear they didn't have much time. They had no water or food.

He wished they had put on his boots in the hospital. Walking on this hard, dusty surface was easy, but not pleasant with only socks on. He supposed he should be glad they hadn't left him in the hospital gown with a diaper on and no back on the gown. That would have been an embarrassing way to die in front of a beautiful doctor.

"How is there light in here?" Joan asked after a few minutes of silent walking.

"Each crystal has an energy we don't understand," Lee said. "Whatever happens, never touch a crystal."

They walked in silence until they left the first big chamber and entered another, almost as big.

"So tell me," Joan said. "Who is this Duster you keep talking about?"

"Duster Kendal," Lee said. "With his wife Bonnie they are two of the greatest math brains in all of the world."

Joan stopped and stared at him.

He walked for a few steps more before stopping and looking back at her.

"Bonnie Kendal funded all my research and gave me the funds to build my building," she said.

Lee nodded. "They do that sort of thing. Ever met them?"

"No," Joan said, starting up again and joining him as they turned to keep walking.

"You'll like them if we can figure a way out of here."

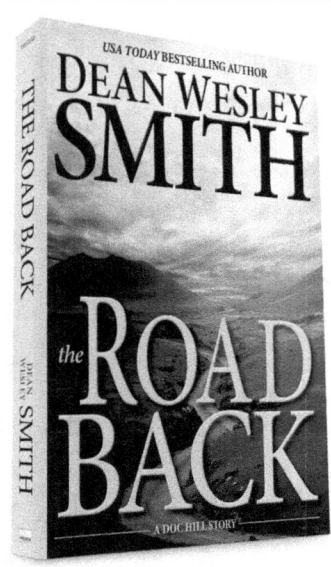

"Seems like you are thinking this is a big if?" Joan said.

"Won't lie to you, doctor," Lee said, not looking at her. "It's a huge if."

At that point they walked on in silence.

FIVE

Time: Unknown
Nexus

JOAN HAD ABOUT a thousand questions because she just flat didn't believe where she was. And who she was walking with.

It was all impossible to believe, actually.

This had to all be a dream and she was going to wake up and laugh at herself and then tell Steph about how she had dreamed Lee Taft was not only awake, but walking and young and handsome. And that they had walked through some beautiful caverns covered in glowing pink crystals.

It could only be a dream.

She and Steph had eaten dinner last night at Carlo's, so clearly next time she needed to avoid eating so much of the wonderful garlic sauce.

But the more they walked, the more this didn't feel like a dream. Other than the fact that everything around her was impossible.

They crossed out of the second cavern and into yet another. The third cavern seemed to be just slightly smaller. She had no idea if that was a good thing or not.

"Let's hope you and I live in some of these timelines around us," Lee said. "No way of knowing for sure, but it would mean we're going in the right direction."

Joan shook her head and decided that even if this was a dream, she needed to know more about how it worked.

"So explain to me how you can travel in timelines?"

Lee shrugged. "Story goes that Duster's family were mining and broke into a cavern close to the surface and in the dimension we live in."

She started to ask what he meant by dimensions, then just shook her head and let him continue.

"Math has proven that energy and time and matter are all linked together, and that math has often said that a manifestation of that link would appear as matter in some way or another."

"The crystals," she said.

"The crystals," he said. "Bonnie and Duster, being brilliant math minds, realized what they had found and after a few years figured out a very simple way to simply step into the past of another timeline. Each timeline is so exactly like the others, it was as if they were stepping back into their own past."

"But they really weren't traveling in time into their own past," Joan said.

"That's right," Lee said. "By going back to the past of another timeline, they created more timelines."

Joan shook her head. She was feeling lost.

Lee saw her shake her head and kept going. "Each crystal is a timeline and when a decision is made, another crystal is formed, both identical except for the decision."

"So my choice of a meal last night at Carlo's caused another timeline?"

She was having a very hard time imagining that.

"Sure," he said. "But if the choice changed nothing, the alternate timeline merged back in with the original. But if the choice was for picking something with a bacteria in it that kills you and picking something safe, then the two timelines would continue on."

"Infinite number of timelines," she said.

"Exactly," he said. "What we are seeing around us are the timelines so close to our own we wouldn't be able to tell the difference."

"That's why the walk?" Joan asked, starting to understand. "The timeline spit us out in an area where you didn't exist? So we have to get back to where you do exist. But if that is the case, what timeline are we in at the moment?"

"My original timeline," Lee said, looking at her with some respect showing in those deep brown eyes. "At least that's what Duster and I figured out would happen."

"So if you had jumped back to the day after your birthday," Joan said, "would this have happened?"

"No," Lee said. "You are pushed sideways into a timeline where you didn't exist. I'm the first to be trapped in a timeline at the time I was being born."

"And holding onto me brought me with you?" Joan asked.

"Yeah, sorry about that again," he said, shaking his head. "I really wasn't thinking. Bringing you along is like clothes or packs. If you are holding them or wearing them, they go with you."

"Luckily Craig dressed you then, isn't it?" Joan asked.

Lee smiled at her and she could see a little of the brilliant Lee Taft behind that smile.

"Very lucky for me."

"So this isn't a dream," she said after they had walked for a few more minutes in silence toward the massive archway into the cavern beyond, climbing slightly as they went across the flat surface.

"I'm afraid it's not," he said.

"So how much trouble are we in?" she asked.

He pointed ahead. "Depends on how far we need to walk and what is there when we reach the end."

"You mean depends on how long we can survive without water."

"Yeah," he said softly. "Afraid so."

PART TWO
The Search

SIX

August 7th, 2018
Central, Idaho

IT TOOK DUSTER about a half hour, pacing himself in the heat and the high altitude, to get to the ranch.

As Duster broke into the meadow with Lee's ranch tucked against the back hill, he paused. From the length of a football field, the place looked completely together. And it would be, since Lee had only left a month or so ago. Duster loved this place.

He stood in the shade of a tree and took a long drink of water. Then headed toward the house.

One key thing was missing. There was no car parked off to one side where Lee always parked. So the tree down hadn't trapped him up here.

As Duster got nearer he could see that even a month with Lee being gone hadn't worn at all on the ranch. Behind the main building, against the rocks, the old wooden-shingled barn stood tall. And where the house was dug into the hill looked normal. Duster knew that was where Lee kept his secret room. It was almost an apartment back there, actually. And that room would be set to explode if anyone tried to get into it.

Duster had no intent to try. With what he had heard from Bonnie about the crystal still being hooked up, he doubted he was going to find Lee here. But he still had to hike up here and look.

Duster took a deep breath and climbed up on the old wooden porch, still solid after over a hundred years. Lee really had put a lot of love and caring into this ranch.

Duster opened the unlocked door to the main house. The ranch house was so tight that not even a film of dust could be seen. The drapes on the windows were pulled closed and Duster left the front door open to let light in.

Duster always had loved coming here to talk with Lee. This ranch felt like a home when Lee was here.

Now, after just sitting empty for a month or so, it was just sad.

More than likely that was just Duster feeling a loss, because if what he thought had happened really did happen, then there was a good chance Lee was never returning to this ranch.

Duster stood near the kitchen table and looked around slowly for anything out of place. Lee had left everything neat and put away. No dishes in the sink, no books left off the large bookshelf that covered one wall. The quilts that Lee always made were folded neatly over the back of the chair and the couch.

Two glasses sat on the coffee table, one in front of Lee's chair, another in front of the couch where Duster always sat. And a bottle of bourbon, Duster's favorite kind, sat between the glasses. The two glasses looked clean and ready to use.

Duster smiled at the fond memory of how many times he and Lee had sat in those same two chairs, sipping bourbon and talking math. Every time Duster had walked through the front door, the two glasses were in their place on the coffee table and a bottle of good bourbon between them.

Damn, Duster hoped he could figure out a way to save his friend.

Lee had left here on purpose. He had left the home he loved with respect, clean and in good order, planning on coming back in just a week or so after a number of trips into the past.

And in another timeline, Lee had left this ranch to head back to the institute to jump to this time. Lee lived in this place in all times. He said it gave him a stability to really focus on the math.

But something must have gone horribly wrong in 1980 between here and the institute in Boise.

If Lee had died, he would have returned to 2018. So something happened to keep him both alive and away from the institute.

And that was the worst scenario any of them could think about.

Duster took a look in the back two rooms just to be sure and then turned and left, closing the door to the ranch with respect, making sure the door was latched.

He stood on the porch and took out his satellite phone.

Bonnie answered instantly.

"He left the place in good shape as he always does," Duster said.

"Something happened to him on the way to the institute," Bonnie said.

"My theory is that he lived until his birthday in May of 1986, but we need to find out for sure what happened. Who do we have that was born after 1986? Get them back there and tracing what happened."

"I'll make sure they don't let him see them or try to rescue him," Bonnie said.

"Good," Duster said. "I'm on my way back to the lodge. See you there for dinner."

He clicked off the phone and put it in the pocket of his jacket. Then he stood and took another long drink of water.

They couldn't rescue Lee before what happened actually happened. If they did, they would only be rescuing him in some timelines and leaving him to die in all the others.

If he actually did die.

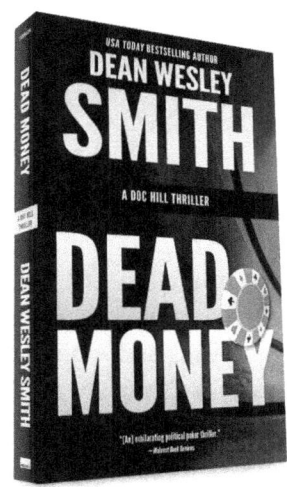

Now Available

**from all your favorite booksellers
in trade paper and electronic editions.**

If they were going to do a rescue, they had to figure out a way to rescue him completely, in all timelines.

Or, in other words, they couldn't do anything to help him that would create other timelines where they didn't do that exact same task.

Duster knew that the bottom line was that Lee had to rescue himself.

Duster shook his head and headed back down the narrow valley to his car. He needed to get up to the lodge and he and Bonnie and Brice and Dixie needed to figure out what they could do to either save Lee or help him.

Duster had a hunch they would all say they could do nothing.

At least until it was clear Lee wasn't going to be able to rescue himself. Then they could save him in a lot of timelines, which would be better than none.

SEVEN

Time: Unknown
Nexus

JOAN AND LEE kept a steady pace for the next five hours, resting only a few minutes each hour. By Lee's count, they had gone through twenty caverns, each one getting smaller and smaller.

He was about as thirsty and hungry as he had ever remembered getting, and at times he felt himself stagger a little. Joan didn't complain, but he knew she had to be as thirsty and hungry as he was.

During the walk he had been surprised at the calmness and clear questions Joan

had asked. He couldn't imagine what condition he would be in if suddenly tossed into this situation. He doubted he would be as calm as she was being.

About two caverns back, after walking for about fifteen minutes without talking, she had asked a simple question. "This isn't a dream, is it?"

He had smiled at her. He could see the fear in her beautiful blue eyes and the strain and dust streaking her wonderful face. He couldn't believe how beautiful she was. And normally with women like her, he seldom talked, but they were in this together. It was his fault she was even here. So he was talking with her and finding as each hour went on he enjoyed it more and more.

She still had on her doctor's smock but it was open showing that she had jeans and tennis shoes and a thin blouse under it. She looked to be in as good a physical shape as he was.

"It's not a dream I'm afraid," he had said. "Would you like to rest?"

"No," she had said.

After six hours of steady walking through cavern after cavern, they finally made it into a cavern that had no exit on the other side.

"Looks like we have reached the end of the road," he said, pointing ahead.

He knew that there was a very high chance they weren't even in the same branch of caverns where Duster's entrance was. If they weren't, they were dead.

This really would be the end of the road for them.

Walking to this cavern had been the only hope he could think of.

"So what are we looking for?" she asked.

"I honestly don't know," he said. "I'm hoping for a door."

They kept walking at a steady pace toward the center of the cavern which felt small compared to some of the massive caverns they had passed through. This one seemed more like a small football stadium instead of a cavern that might cover a city.

About halfway across, he spotted what he had been hoping to find.

"There," he said. He wanted to do a dance with relief, but didn't.

A dark metal door seemed to mar the perfect surface of the crystals. It looked tiny down at ground level, which gave him an idea of just how far away they still were.

Somehow, even though he wanted to run, they kept the same pace until they reached the area of the door.

"This isn't a good sign," he said, pointing to a pile covered in the cavern fine dirt about twenty steps from the door. It was the first mound of anything they had seen in all the flat-floored caverns.

"What is it?" she asked.

Duster once told me that when they first jumped into other timelines, they left from this cavern. They had a wooden table here."

He pointed to the pile of dirt.

"What happened to it?" she asked.

"It crumbled with age I would bet," Lee said.

"How long would that take?" Joan asked, turning those wonderful and very panicked brown eyes on him.

"Three hundred to five hundred years or more, maybe," Lee said. "No real weather in here to help it along."

Joan just looked puzzled.

"Duster and I both theorized that time is not the same in these caverns as in the real world," he said. "We are, more than likely, hundreds and hundreds of years past our normal time."

"Oh, this nightmare just gets worse and worse," she said, shaking her head.

"I'm afraid I have to agree with you there," Lee said, turning and heading toward the metal door. He just hoped it was unlocked or at least deteriorated enough that they could get through it.

"Remember," he said, "Don't touch the crystals."

"Not thinking about it," she said.

The handle to the rusted metal door was built into the sheet of metal and when he pulled on it, it didn't seem to want to open.

Near the entrance the crystals had been cleared back a few feet, so he braced one dirt-covered foot against the stone and then pulled.

The door complained with a screeching sound that echoed through the cavern, then opened enough for them to get through.

He tried to open it more, but that was all it would go.

He slid through first and into what looked like an old mining tunnel. The only light was from the crystals in the cavern behind them.

"You need to let me go first," Joan said. "I have shoes on and the last thing we need is you stepping on some rusty metal."

He was about to object but realized she was right and let her move past him and into the pitch black of whatever was beyond.

"Hang on a minute," he said.

He braced his back against the side of the tunnel and then with one foot against the metal door, pushed as hard as he could.

Again the door complained but opened wider, letting in even more light.

He moved to follow close behind her as they went down the tunnel not more than ten steps before it opened into a large cave.

The moment Joan stepped into the cave, lights came up.

"Oh, thank god," she said, her breathing hard and heavy. "I hate dark, closed-in places."

"That makes two of us," he said.

Other than the dim lights on the ceiling, many of which had clearly burnt out, the big cavern was empty.

"I remember Duster telling me there used to be a kitchen and bathrooms to the back of this room to the right."

They both started in that direction and it became clear that the counter outline on the floor was still there. But everything had been removed a long, long time ago.

They split up and moved around the empty cavern, slowly trying to find anything that might help them. It was Joan who found the clock.

"Lee, over here," she said.

She was staring at a clock embedded in one stone wall.

"It's an atomic clock," he said as he moved up beside her.

Lee stared at the clock for a moment, then just slowly whistled.

It was seven in the morning of September 6th, 2728.

"We are so screwed," Joan said softly.

Lee couldn't argue with that.

EIGHT

September 6th, 2728
Near the Nexus

THEY STOOD THERE for a moment, staring at the clock, neither one of them speaking. Lee was used to traveling in time, but seven hundred years ahead of when he left was something even he was having trouble grasping. He couldn't imagine how Joan was feeling.

Finally, he turned from the clock and looked around the empty room. "We need to get out of here, find food and water."

Joan nodded and turned to face him. "Any idea how?"

Lee nodded and turned for the far side of the large cave. "Duster said his distant relatives dug a mine that broke into the cavern. We need to find the mine tunnel."

"Can't imagine a mine tunnel after seven hundred years still being open," Joan said.

"I can't imagine that Duster didn't make sure it couldn't collapse," Lee said. "And they would have had to come back here at times to get more crystals and return the ones used at the institute."

"I didn't see any piles of crystals out there," Joan said.

Lee just nodded to that. He hadn't either and that had bothered him. But he didn't tell her that.

The old mine tunnel was easy to spot on the other side of the cavern and it looked secure, even though the big timbers were made of wood.

It was wide enough for two of them to walk side-by-side and tall enough that Lee felt he didn't have to duck under any of the timbers. It smelled damp and cold and moldy.

As Lee eased into the tunnel, lights came up showing him the way ahead. He had no idea what kind of power was running the lights, but most of the bulbs were out, clearly showing no one had done any upkeep on this place in a very, very long time.

"Have I told you how much I hate closed-in places," Joan said, moving along slowly beside him.

"Yeah, can't imagine how anyone worked in a place like this," Lee said.

They finally reached what was clearly the end of the tunnel. A large metal door was on the right side and ahead of them it looked like rocks had caved in the tunnel.

"Duster said there was an airlock and hidden entrance to the mine," Lee said. "To make sure no light got out when they went in and out at night."

Lee pushed a large red button and with a groan the metal door slid into the wall, showing a small chamber.

"We go in there and the door closes and then doesn't open," Joan said, "we're dead."

"We're going to die if we don't get out of here and find water and food," Lee said. "Running out of oxygen in there would be quicker."

"I don't even like my walk-in closet at home," Joan said. Then she took a deep breath and said, "Let's do it."

Lee nodded.

She took his hand and they stepped into the small space on the other side of the metal door.

Lee liked the feel of her hand in his and surprisingly, it calmed him.

As they stood inside, nothing happened. The door behind them didn't close.

Then Lee saw the other button on the wall. He hit it.

"Oh, shit," Joan said as the door behind them slid closed with a thud.

Total blackness.

"This is not fun," Lee said.

Joan's hand squeezed his as a moaning sound of machinery trying to work reached them and finally the large wall in front of them slid sideways.

The cold bite of morning air hit them in the face. The sun was just coloring some high clouds in the sky. It was going to be a beautiful day from the looks of it.

The air smelled dry and had a tint of dry pine to it.

In front of them was a small ledge about five feet wide and not much else. They were a pretty good distance up on the side of a very large mountain. It wasn't a cliff, but the hill going down wasn't something Lee wanted to try to get down.

With Joan's hand in his, they eased out onto the dirt ledge that now looked to be part of something that had been bigger, more than likely mine tailings. Behind them the mountain rumbled and a large rock slid closed over the entrance, hiding it completely.

Joan took a deep breath and then said simply, "Thank heavens."

Lee wasn't happy that they were now cut off from the crystals. But there really hadn't been anything back there for them anyway. Food and water were becoming critical. Survival was first, then trying to figure out how to get back to 2018 would be second.

To the left of where they stood there was a wider area and Lee squeezed Joan's hand and led the way in that direction.

She didn't seem to want to let go of his hand yet and honestly, he didn't want her to.

But once they reached the wider, brush-covered area, she did finally let go, looking around at the tree-covered mountains and the deep valley below them, taking deep breaths and working to calm down.

"Any idea where we are?"

"Owyhee Mountains," Lee said. "Ever heard of an old ghost town by the name of Silver City?"

She nodded.

He pointed down to the dark valley below them. "It used to be down there. Can't imagine anything being left now after seven hundred years."

"Think there might be water down there?" Joan said.

Lee nodded. "I think there might be some we could wash up in, but I don't think we should drink any of it. We would be safer getting over that ridge there and down onto the Snake River to find clean water."

He pointed at the ridge across the deep valley. It actually wasn't a ridge. That was War Eagle Mountain. But even if the roads were gone in here, they could get past the mountain and down on the Snake River.

"You familiar with this area?" Joan asked, turning to look at him.

He nodded. "Spent a lot of time with my father up here hunting deer when I was young. I can get us to the Snake River. What we find there will help us decide what to do next."

She nodded, staring out over the valley as slowly the sun started to hit the tops of the mountains.

"It's beautiful, isn't it?"

"It really is," she said, nodding. "But hard to appreciate when I'm this thirsty and hungry."

"Then let's go find some food and water," he said, smiling at her.

He picked his way past her and up on a trail that looked like it would lead over to a ridgeline they could get down. Doing this without shoes was going to be tough.

Painfully tough.

But he really had no choice.

NINE

September 6th, 2728
Snake River in Owyhee County, Idaho

JEAN WAS STUNNED at how tough Lee was. He didn't complain, just kept on moving, even though it became clear as each hour went by that his feet were hurting. And his black socks looked like they were caking with blood.

And she knew he was as hungry as she was, maybe more so. She had at least had a decent breakfast what seemed like a long time ago. Actually, it had been a long time. More than seven hundred years ago, actually.

She was finding that hard to grasp.

Luckily for them the day hadn't turned out to be sunny or that hot. If it had been, she doubted they would have made it as far as they had.

She glanced at Lee who seemed to walk with pride, even though every step must have been pure agony.

She was finding it hard to grasp that a man she only knew from being in a coma for six years, who had had a broken back, was now leading her along what looked to be an old paved highway gone to seed.

In some places trees fifty or more years old grew from the pavement.

By Joan's watch, if it could still be trusted, it had taken them six hours to climb down off that first mountain, climb back up over a second ridge and then make their way along an old road down to this paved road. They hadn't talked much since there wasn't much to talk about.

They needed food and they needed water.

That was the focus.

There hadn't even been water in the creek in the bottom of the valley to tempt them.

The old paved road being left to go to seed bothered her more than she wanted to admit and finally, after about thirty minutes of walking along the road, weaving in and around trees and brush growing up through it, she had to ask Lee his opinion.

"Did you expect this kind of state of disrepair?"

He shrugged and kept walking. "Lots of reasons for it. A new road built somewhere else, or ground cars are not needed in 2728."

She laughed. "I went right to the worst case reason," she said.

Lee nodded. "I went there at first myself. Not sure why I think civilization wouldn't survive a short seven hundred years. But I did. Interesting that we both did."

"So any theories why the mine wasn't maintained?"

"I wish I had one," he said. "I know that Duster and some of the other founders of the institute are actually set in 2318. What I mean by that is they were taken forward in time in the same manner I took you with me, and so when they travel back, only two minutes pass in 2318 even though they live full lives in the past. So I would have thought they would have just kept the institute going forward in time until now and beyond. I'm sure hoping they did."

They walked in silence for a moment as she tried to make sense of that.

Finally, she decided to ask the question that she had wanted to ask since he first explained things in the caverns.

"Was the trip you fell off the horse your first trip back into the past?"

Lee shook his head. "Nope. It was the 35th full trip."

"Full trip?"

"I always jump first back to 1890 and build my ranch up in central Idaho. I stay there and do research until 1920, then jump back, turning around using the same crystal, the same timeline, and going back to 1925. I would stay on my ranch then until 1950. Then back to 2018 before returning to 1955 to stay until 1980. I call that a full trip."

Joan just sort of walked in stunned silence. Her stomach had long since given up reminding her she needed to eat and she felt so thirsty, she wasn't sure how much farther she could go. Now the man she was with was telling her he lived for eighty years in the same ranch and had done that thirty-five times.

If she hadn't already been through so much, she would be laughing.

At that moment, as the road turned to the left, he pointed to the right and picked his way down a slight embankment and into some pine trees.

She followed, not liking that they were now off the road and going cross-country somewhere. But Lee sure seemed to know where he was going, so she didn't question him. She had lived in Idaho her entire life and had never once bothered to even visit this part of the state.

After a few minutes they broke out of the trees. They were standing on a cliff face looking out over a huge river.

"Snake River," Lee said. "Isn't it beautiful?"

Joan just stood there, staring, her mouth open. Beautiful didn't begin to describe that river. She could see for a few miles upstream as it wound its way down a lush valley and then disappeared to the left around a bend just past where they stood. The water was clear and blue and the smell was of a damp clay.

"Now be careful," Lee said.

He took her hand and led her along the rocks to a trail that led down along the cliff.

"Focus on where you put your feet," he said, moving ahead of her but keeping a tight grip on her hand. "You don't want to slip."

She was far less afraid of heights as she was of dark, enclosed places. But this still suddenly got her very tired mind and body focused.

Sharply focused.

She wasn't sure she could climb down the entire cliff, but after twenty feet, it was clear she wasn't going to have to.

A wide ledge, about the size of her office, jutted out of the cliff face. It had a few small pine trees growing up on one side in the rocks, a large natural pool against some rocks, and from the rocks near them a bubbling stream made

the most wonderful sound she had ever heard.

"Only a sip to start with," Lee said as they moved to the spring.

As a doctor she knew that, but was still very glad he had warned her.

He first splashed water on his face and then took a small sip.

Standing beside him, she did the same.

The feeling of the ice-cold water on her face was like nothing she had ever felt before.

Nothing.

And that first sip was heavenly. The best drink of anything in her life. And something she would always remember.

TEN

September 6th, 2728
Snake River in Owyhee County, Idaho

LEE SPLASHED WATER on his face and then washed off his arms and neck and hair, carefully sipping only tiny amounts of water each minute or so.

Beside him Joan did the same. For the first time she took off her white lab jacket and really washed her face and arms as well.

"Wish we had something to eat with this," she said.

"We do," he said, "but we need to climb back up and pick it, then come down here again to rest."

He took one last small sip of water, then led the way, holding her hand again, back up the short twenty feet to the forest above them.

He took a few steps back into the pine and found what he had seen on the way through. Pine cones from what were called single-leaf pinyon pines.

He picked up the cone and studied it, seeing the nuts just under the spines of the cone.

The pinyon pines didn't grow in the area of his ranch in central Idaho, but here along the Snake River and down into northern Utah, they were all over the place. Native Americans used to eat the nuts as part of their diet and for a time in the early west, export places sent the nuts around the world.

"Pine nuts?" she said.

"Actually pretty good," he said. "And good protein, but we didn't dare eat them without water in our systems."

She nodded at that.

He started gathering up cones and handing them to her. She had put back on her lab jacket, so she stuffed them in her pockets.

After they had about ten cones full of more nuts than they dared eat in the next day, he moved over to an area along the cliff face and picked some fresh-looking dandelions. He didn't much like the flavor of them, but he was starving and had little choice at the moment.

"Now I know people eat those," she said, nodding as she picked some as well and stuffed them in her pockets.

Then they headed back down the cliff, again going slowly. When they reached the spring they both took another small sip of water.

They put the dandelions and pinecones next to the pool of water.

He pointed to the top half of the pool. "Hot springs come in there, water from the cold springs comes down here. Hundreds of years ago this used to be the perfect temperature to soak in."

She reached down and touched the water, then smiled. "Like a warm bath."

"Wonderful thing about Mother Nature," he said, peeling off his shirt. "It takes a long time for things to change."

He sat down beside the pool and then carefully and painfully pulled off his socks. Luckily he had very few cuts. Mostly his feet were bruised and bruised badly.

Joan had removed her lab coat again and came over to check his feet. She nodded a few times. "They could be a lot worse, considering the ground you covered in only socks."

"Yeah," he said. "But right now they feel like rocks tied to my ankles."

"Soak them and clean them for a little while," she said. "But not too long in the water."

"Thanks, doc," he said, smiling at her.

With that she stood above him and started taking off her shoes and then her pants.

Underwear and all.

Then she pulled her blouse over her head and was standing there completely naked.

She was the most beautiful woman he had ever seen. Small breasts, blonde pubic hair, not an ounce of fat on her anywhere.

"You think if I washed the blouse and socks," she said, picking them up without an ounce of modesty, "they would dry?"

It took him a moment, but he nodded. "Still warm out here and that slight breeze along the river will dry them in no time."

She nodded, then waded into the pool, making all kinds of wonderful sounds of pleasure as she sank into the water.

"Come on in, the water's great."

He nodded, but he felt clearly embarrassed. In all his years of life, he had never been naked in front of a woman before. He had lost his virginity back in college and had a few girlfriends, but they always seemed to be more trouble than they were worth.

She could sense his hesitation, clearly.

She smiled. "Remember, I've seen you naked already."

He looked at her, puzzled.

"You were in a coma for six years."

He laughed, clearly feeling his face blush.

"I bet I've seen places on you that you haven't seen."

He started to open his mouth, then shut it and just shook his head.

"Helped change your diaper a few times as well," she said, smiling.

He could feel his face turning completely red. Then her smile got to him and he laughed.

"How about we never mention that again," he said.

"Deal," she said, smiling.

With that he stood and pulled off his pants, shorts and all, then his shirt as she watched. And he honestly didn't mind that she was watching.

Then he slid carefully into the pool beside the most beautiful woman he could have ever imagined being beside.

ELEVEN

September 6th, 2728
Snake River in Owyhee County, Idaho

JOAN WAS SHOCKED at how seeing Lee healthy and naked was so different than seeing Lee the patient. She had never realized how good of shape he was in.

And when he had been her patient, he had been twenty-five plus years older as well.

Now he was an amazingly in-shape, handsome man. She couldn't do anything

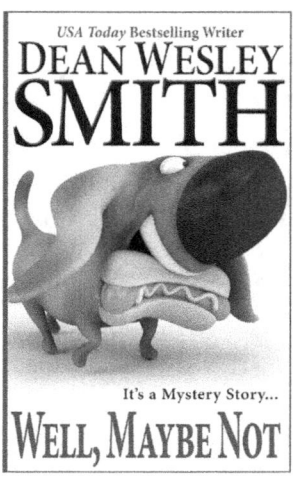

but stare as he carefully worked his way into the pool.

After they both got completely washed off, they went to work on the pine cones. For a while she stayed in the pool, pulling out the small nuts and putting them on a rock near the edge. But that got awkward, so she just got out and sat on a stone on the edge and worked at the cones there.

Lee did the same, sitting naked on a rock beside her.

It felt completely natural and wonderful. A mountain hot springs, a warm afternoon, a slight breeze that brought them the smell of hot pine trees and of the river below. If they weren't so far from home and starving, she might have actually enjoyed it a lot more.

In fact, she knew she would have.

The sips of water they had managed to get down had upset her stomach only for a moment, and as she took more and more water, she could feel the thirst starting to abate and the hunger take over.

"We need to make sure we chew these up really, really well," Lee said. "Then swallow them with just a little bit of water."

She understood that. The wilderness way of things was exactly as she would have directed for a patient in the hospital in their conditions.

"How many?" she asked.

"I think we should start with about five, see how that goes."

She put five of the nuts in her mouth and chewed them until they were pulp. They were easy to chew, just as with any raw nut, and they actually had a bland cashew flavor. She could see how roasted with a little salt these would have been popular.

She swallowed them with a tiny sip of water.

Lee did the same, then they both washed some clothes. He washed his socks completely, banging them a few times on a smooth rock. And his underwear and his shirt.

She washed her underwear, her blouse, and her socks.

They hung the clothes on branches on one of the small pine trees so that the wind and sun would dry them, then went back to have seconds on the pine nuts.

She was starting to feel almost human again.

Almost.

And clearly Lee looked like he was feeling better as well, even though he was limping.

After their third helping of nuts, they both got back into the pool for a while.

"I can't tell you how sorry I am about getting you into all this," Lee said as they settled into the water.

She laughed. "Tell you what, you stop apologizing for that and I'll never mention the coma stuff again."

He laughed. "Deal."

He shook her hand on that, which honestly felt wonderful. She was seven hundred years in the future, on the edge of starving and was having feelings for the naked man beside her in the pool.

It hadn't been that long since her last boyfriend, had it?

"This pool feels better than I remember," he said.

"You here with a woman the first time as well?" Joan asked.

"Nope," he said. "By myself. Just out of my last year of my doctorate. Came up here to scatter my father's ashes where he loved to hunt. Duster told me about this and how to find it."

She didn't want to say anything about his father, so she asked the next question. "What field did you get your doctorate in?"

"First one was for applied physics. Second one the mathematical theory of time."

He said that so matter-of-factly, all she could do was stare.

"And you built a ranch back in the past to study time?" she asked. "Why do that?"

"I am studying the influences of travelers like myself, and now you, on timelines," he said. "I needed to try to keep a low footprint myself in the past to really be able to see the influences that others left, at least mathematically, across a wide range of alternate timelines. A whole lot of mathematical theory, mostly."

"Oh," was all she could say.

"I am making progress, actually. Hope we can get out of this so I can report to Bonnie and Duster about my findings."

"I hope we can get out of this as well," she said. "But for other reasons."

Lee laughed and nodded and then stared out over the river valley below

She just watched his handsome face. She had a hunch that if anyone could get them out of this mess, it would be Lee.

She hadn't known the awake Lee very long, but the longer she knew him, the more she felt comfortable with him.

And not as afraid.

TWELVE

September 7th, 2728
Snake River in Owyhee County, Idaho

LEE WAS VERY happy the afternoon and evening had gone as well as it had. They had managed to keep down about ten helpings of pine nuts, a bunch

of dandelions, and enough water that they both ended up peeing again, which meant they were getting hydrated.

As the sun set, they had gotten dressed. He really felt comfortable being naked with Joan and watching her wonderful body, but they didn't dare get chilled going into the night.

They had decided they would stay on the wide ledge near the pool until morning because it was just safer from animals than back up in the trees. There was no sign any animals used the pool for drinking. He figured that the river below them was too close for the animals to bother with this pool.

The night wasn't going to be cold, but it wasn't going to be warm either. So they had built a stone wall around where they would sleep to block any wind.

Then they had both just lay there, using her lab coat as a light blanket, staring at the stars through the passing clouds above. No moon tonight yet, so what stars they could see were bright.

After a while, when the sky was totally dark, he had sat up and looked over the river to the north.

No lights.

That had been his worst fear when he had seen no crystals stacked in the room outside the door and now it was coming true.

Joan had sat up beside him. "Something wrong?"

"No lights," he had said.

"No lights from what?" she had asked.

"From the entire Treasure Valley. Boise alone should light up the sky in that direction. It did when I was here by myself seven hundred years ago."

"Oh, no," she had said.

Oh, no was right. In the last hundreds of years something horrible had happened. And they were walking right into it.

He had touched her arm and they stretched out again, but he only slept a little through the night. Instead he had just stared at the dark sky in the distance.

In the morning, as the sun colored the sky orange over the ridges to the east, they both ate more nuts and drank their share of water. They had nothing they could carry water in, but they could take nuts with them.

So when they went back up the cliff to the trees, they spent a half hour getting more nuts from cones and filling their pockets with them.

His feet were again just dead-feeling hunks on the bottom of his ankles. He was going to need to figure out something to cover them.

By the time they reached the road, he was really hobbling.

Joan had him stop and she ripped some strips off the bottom of her lab coat and tied them around his feet, giving the soles of his feet far more padding than his socks did.

"Not sure why I didn't think about doing that before now," she said.

"Not sure why I hadn't thought of it either," he said.

That felt a lot better, almost as if he had shoes on.

"So where are we heading?" Joan asked as they started off down the overgrown road.

He glanced at her. She looked refreshed and beautiful in the morning light. She was a brilliant woman, of that there was no doubt.

"I'm thinking we try to eventually reach the institute in Boise," he said. "Only chance we have of getting back to our own time. If the institute is still there."

She nodded. "What's ahead of us today? Never been in this part of the state before."

"There was a bridge across the river about three miles ahead," he said. "We'll join a main highway shortly."

"I hope the bridge is still standing," she said.

"Yeah, me too. And beyond the bridge are a few small farming towns. I got a hunch we'll get some answers there."

"And maybe find you some shoes," she said.

"We can only hope," Lee said, smiling at her.

Just over an hour later they reached the bridge. It clearly was hundreds of years old and looked more functional than anything else, made of metal and mostly flat. The main road was clearly in as bad of shape as the road they had been on, but the bridge was still standing, but not by much. Another decade or two of hard winters and high water and the rusted metal bridge would only be a memory.

Now Available
**from all your favorite booksellers
in trade paper and electronic editions.**

From the looks of the road, he and Joan might just end up being the last two humans to ever cross the bridge. The highway sure wasn't passable anymore.

A mile down the road they could see the trees and buildings of what looked like a small town.

They were going to have some answers soon.

Or at least he hoped they would.

One way or another.

THIRTEEN

September 7th, 2728
Snake River in Owyhee County, Idaho

JOAN HAD NEVER felt so afraid before as they got closer to what looked like a small town.

The morning had turned out to be a warm, but not a hot morning, with a slight breeze along the river that kept her feeling actually comfortable.

And sadly, there were enough pine trees and scrub trees growing on and along the highway that they had stayed in the shade a large amount of the walk.

Lee seemed to be just ignoring his feet, but he couldn't keep doing that for long.

"So tell me," she said, "everything was fine in 2318, right?"

"Yes," Lee said. "And I never asked Duster why they didn't keep going forward or why they had stopped at 2318. Question never came up, so maybe they didn't and I just paid no attention."

"So this is 2728," she said, trying to calm herself and make herself relax some before they walked into that town they could see ahead. "That's four hundred years plus."

"Humans could have made great strides in that amount of time," she said. "So much so that roads like this aren't needed anymore."

"Possible," he said. "But other things worry me as well."

He pointed to what had clearly been a very good piece of farmland to the left of the road along a flat area just above the river. Trees and brush had taken it over and completely reclaimed it.

She nodded and looked ahead. "I don't think I'm going to like what we are about to find."

"I'm kind of hoping to find a pair of old shoes," he said, smiling at her.

She laughed. "Yeah, that would be nice."

Fifteen minutes later they walked down the center of the old road between six buildings, three on each side of the road. One had been a café, one a grocery store, another some form of shop. One was a house, one looked like an old stone county office building that looked like it was built back in the early 1900s.

They were all clearly abandoned and in bad shape.

"This looks like it was abandoned only about a hundred years or so ago," Lee said. "A lot of the buildings still have windows."

"This valley must be sheltered from storms," she said.

"Which building first?" he asked.

She glanced around at the buildings. "The home. Best chance of finding you some shoes."

He nodded and they started toward the house. It had a flat, long feel to it, with a roof of some strange black substance

and what looked to be wood siding, but she doubted it actually was.

It had the feel of a futuristic home echoing back to a 1970s manufactured house.

Near the front door, she stopped him. "I'm going to go in first because the last thing at this moment we need is you stepping on some broken glass or anything else for that matter."

She could see he was about to object, but she shook her head. "Let me look first. It's not going to kill you to stand here, but it might kill you to go in there."

He nodded and she turned for the door, climbing up the three concrete steps.

She felt like she should knock, then laughed and just tried the fake wooden door.

It opened easily, swinging inward.

Inside was what looked to be some sort of modern furniture like she had never seen before filling a living room to the left of the door and what she was sure was a kitchen straight ahead.

Odd shapes, strange pastel colors, nothing like she had seen in her time. It had a sense of being lived in, though.

Everything was covered in a thick layer of gray dust and the entire place smelled musty and dead.

She glanced around the floor, then motioned that Lee should join her.

"No glass," she said. "But watch every step."

He nodded, then said, "Yes, doc."

She turned and slowly headed for what looked like a kitchen. There was a dining table to one side, covered in some yellowed papers and a few small mechanical devices of some sort or another.

"Wow, way beyond modern," Lee said.

He moved carefully over to what seemed like a cabinet drawer and opened it.

"Knives and things we can use," he said, smiling as he held one up.

"Medical and shoes is what we could really use," she said.

"I'll keep looking here," he said. "You try some of the other rooms."

She nodded and turned away from him. Even though this home had clearly been built hundreds of years after her time, it still had the standard structure of a ranch house, with rooms down a very wide hallway. Guess no one had improved much on that basic design for human living.

The first room to her right looked like a small bathroom. Toilet was strangely shaped, but it was clearly still a toilet.

She moved on to the next open door on the right. A bedroom. Empty of anything but a bed and what appeared to be a closed closet.

Moving carefully, she went to the open door on the left. This room was considerably larger and had a large bed against the far wall.

It took her a moment to register what she was seeing in the bed.

A human skull and hair on one of the pillows.

And a second skull and hair on the pillow beside it.

Her stomach twisted up into a knot. So much for humans just advancing to the place they didn't need to be in this area.

"Lee!"

As a doctor, she wasn't afraid of seeing death and had seen it many times. But seeing these two people, dead and still in their bed scared her more than she wanted to admit.

A moment later he joined her in the wide doorway, then said simply, "Shit."

She moved toward the bed, moving slowly. The room only smelled musty,

which meant these two had been dead for a very, very long time.

She studied the skulls. All skin had long ago dried away. From just the hair and sizes of bumps they made in the blanket, one looked to be a man, the other a small-framed woman.

She looked around at how the light came in and if there was any air movement in the bedroom. One window was slightly open and blinds still hung from the window.

So there had been air movement in the room. The heat of the summer days, the dampness of the winter nights, had all had a chance to work on these bodies.

"Any idea how long ago this happened?" Lee asked.

"Got to be at least a hundred years would be my guess," she said.

"Look at this," Lee said and pointed to a spot beside the bed.

Curled on what looked to have been a blanket was the skeleton of a dog, its dark hair forming a pile around the bones and skull.

"Whatever happened to the people was very sudden and killed animals as well," Lee said.

"And some insects," Joan said, trying to stay in her doctor analytical mind-set. "Notice any spiders in here? And I haven't seen a bug anywhere."

Lee glanced around, shaking his head. "I haven't noticed even a single insect the entire time."

They stood in silence near the bed of the dead couple.

She knew that most insects, bees, and birds were major ways that plants exchanged pollen, but the plants that required that would have died off as well a hundred years ago and only the plants that pollen was carried on the winds would have survived.

What could have killed people and animals and insects instantly as they slept? And left everything else alone completely?

"I think I need some air," she said finally, turning and heading for the door. Her cold, calm scientist brain was about to slip and she could feel it.

"I think that's a damn good idea," he said.

Together, they went back out and sat on the front steps of the home, looking at the dead highway in front of them.

She just wanted to scream. But she had no doubt that would be a worthless thing to do.

But she still wanted to do it.

PART THREE
Trail of Death

FOURTEEN

August 7th, 2018
Central, Idaho

DUSTER DECIDED TO let Brice and Dixie stay in Boise instead of coming up to the meeting in the Monumental Lodge. They wanted to crunch numbers there on the big institute computer to try to figure out approximately where Lee would have ended up.

So joining Duster for dinner in the back room of the lodge was Director Parks and Bonnie and Dawn Edwards.

Dawn and her husband, Madison, were two of his closest friends. Madison also had stayed in Boise to help out there. Lee vanishing had all hands on deck.

In the two hours it had taken Duster to drive back up to the lodge that occupied a ridgeline high in the Idaho central mountains and taken a quick shower and get into the dining room, Bonnie and Director Parks had arrived by helicopter. Dawn was already at the lodge, since she ran it and lived there all year long.

The lodge made Duster feel at home. He and Bonnie and Dawn and Madison had built it in 1902 so many times in so many timelines, he had lost count. The huge polished log beams and log walls and the furniture original to the 1900 time period gave the place a feeling of timelessness.

The back dining room was only used for their meetings.

Bonnie had ordered him a steak with baked potatoes and an iced tea and the tea was already at his spot at the long wood table when he arrived.

He kissed Bonnie and nodded to Parks and Dawn. All three of them looked very serious.

Bonnie looked as radiant as ever, with her long brown hair pulled back. She had on a golden silk blouse and jeans. He couldn't believe that after so many thousands and thousands of years together, they could still be in such deep love. In fact, it seemed to grow stronger and stronger. They had often spent decades apart, but when together, he felt stronger with her beside him.

And Parks looked like he always looked, dressed in jeans and a dress shirt with his sleeves rolled up. His brown hair was cut short, as always, and even though he managed the institute over a six-hundred-year period, he didn't seem the worse for wear. And he never seemed stressed.

Duster had no idea how he managed that.

Dawn also looked as she seemed to always look from century to century. She was short compared to Bonnie and kept her dark hair pulled back. She wore a comfortable cotton blouse and jeans.

A person coming into this room would never be able to tell that the four of them were thousands of years old and had more advanced degrees than they could count.

"So the ranch showed no signs Lee had been there in the last month or so?" Bonnie asked.

Duster nodded and sipped the iced tea. "He hasn't returned. So what happened to him?"

"We sent back four people familiar with 1980s time and who would not be born until after 1990 to trail him," Parks said.

"He fell off his horse just outside of Cascade," Parks said, glancing at his notes. "He was leading a second horse into a ranch there where he had made arrangements to sell the horses. From a witness at the ranch, it looked as if a snake spooked the horse and it reared suddenly."

"They got to him quickly," Bonnie said, "but he had a head injury and had broken his back."

"They airlifted him to Boise and saved his life," Parks said, "but he remained in a coma at the Failor Clinic for six years."

Duster glanced at Bonnie. "We fund that place?"

"We do," Bonnie said, nodding. "Even though it is a little before our time."

"From what we can tell," Parks said, again glancing down at notes in his hand, "he woke up from the six-year coma the morning of his actual birthday. Brice and Dixie are trying to figure out why that happened. They figure it was some sort of time pressure."

Duster nodded.

"At the moment of his birth across town in a Boise hospital, he vanished out of his bed at the Failor Clinic."

"But didn't return to the institute crystal," Duster said, nodding.

They had always theorized that might happen to someone who tried to stay past their own birthday in a timeline. The person wouldn't return to the timeline crystal because they had been pushed out of that timeline. Time wouldn't let anyone be alive in the same timeline at the same moment in history.

"Brice and Dixie think he was dumped in the caverns," Parks said.

Bonnie nodded. "More than likely near crystals of timelines where he didn't exist."

Duster nodded. That had been their theory as to what would happen and it seemed to be playing out.

"But we have another problem," Parks said.

Duster couldn't imagine another problem being this bad, so he said nothing and let Parks continue.

"It seems, from what one of our people said, that Lee learned about the time and date just slightly before his birth time," Parks said.

Duster nodded.

Parks actually looked embarrassed that he was about to report what happened, so Bonnie broke in.

"He grabbed Dr. Failor," Bonnie said. "Lee was trying to convince her that he needed to get to the institute."

"Oh, no," Duster said, his stomach twisting. "He took her with him."

Bonnie and Parks and Dawn all nodded.

"It's a real mess," Parks said.

"We think we have it contained," Bonnie said.

"Major timeline changes?" Duster asked, not sure if he really wanted to know the answer.

"Brice and Dixie are running the math on that right now," Parks said, "as well as trying to figure out where in the caverns Lee and Dr. Failor might have ended up."

"How far in the future you mean?" Duster asked.

"Exactly," Parks said.

"More than likely," Bonnie said, staring at Duster, "they are a ways after the event."

Duster nodded and sat back, trying to make sense of what he had been told.

Nothing about this was good. Nothing at all.

The event was a point in time in the future when all human and animal and insect life had been wiped out by, from what they could figure out, a massive blast of some sort of energy from space.

And now, with Lee and Dr. Failor beyond the point in time, that event, every option to rescue them might cause even more damage, if that was possible.

And it certainly wouldn't save Lee and Dr. Failor.

Or at least not all of them in all timelines.

FIFTEEN

September 7th, 2728
Old Highway 45, Southern Idaho

LEE AND JOAN sat on the concrete house steps for a good fifteen minutes, then got up and went back inside the home to look for anything that might help them to survive and get to Boise.

Their only hope of getting out of this was to get to the institute. And making that hike was not going to be easy.

Former PGA Golf Professional and USA Today *bestselling writer Dean Wesley Smith walks you step-by-step, club-by-club from your car to the first tee and beyond in a laugh-out-loud style that not only teaches, but entertains.*

A perfect gift for the golfer in your family.

Now Available
from all your favorite booksellers in trade paper and electronic editions.

They needed something to carry water. And they were going to somehow have to figure out how to get more food.

And he needed something to protect his feet.

Most of the clothes the couple had in their closets fell apart when touched. But the synthetic fiber clothing that had been kept in the dark away from any elements seemed fine.

From the size of the guy's feet and coats, he had been bigger than Lee. But a pair of the guy's boots seemed to still be holding together pretty well, so he and Joan managed to get a few layers of socks on Lee's feet and get the boots on tight enough for him to walk.

It actually felt heavenly having padding and the boots taking a lot of the shock of each step.

They mostly worked in silence, not talking, just working together as a team as if they had done that for years. Lee was very impressed at how Joan was doing with all this. At times she seemed to be in better shape than he was.

The woman had been about Joan's size, so Joan found a light raincoat and a second pair of tennis shoes that seemed like they might hold together for a little while.

They found two synthetic backpacks tucked in another closet. So by the time they left that house, Lee had boots that would protect his feet until he could find something better, pocketknives, matches that still lit, and glass containers to carry water. And both had raincoats in case they needed those.

They also each carried a light blanket.

Lee had grabbed a small crowbar as well and had it hanging on his pack. There was no telling where they might have to break into a place. In fact, he had no idea exactly what lay ahead of them.

As they set off along the road out of the small town, headed for Boise, Joan turned to him. "We're going to need to find water."

"If I remember correctly," Lee said, "over the next hill there is a small river or large stream the road crosses."

"Are we going to be able to drink it safely?"

Lee nodded. "Pretty sure we are. If animals were killed at the same time as humans by whatever did this, the streams will be running fairly clean after a hundred years."

Joan nodded.

Lee made himself walk purposefully in the larger boots, making sure he got the heel of each foot down first. It would take a little training to get used to walking in these, but it was a lot better than not having anything but socks on. A thousand times better.

After about a half mile of walking in silence, Joan glanced at Lee.

"Help me understand a few things about this traveling in other timelines."

Lee glanced at her and smiled. "I'll try."

"Can you go into the future of another timeline?"

"No," Lee said. "Timelines, thus more crystals, are being created by every decision in the world. You can only go backwards in an existing crystal timeline."

She nodded. "So how did your friends get into the future from your timeline?"

"Someone from the time in the future came back and got them and moved them forward," Lee said. "That's what happened to me. Director Parks of the institute took me forward three jumps of one hundred years each by holding onto me as I held onto you."

"I'm confused," Joan said as they crested a hill. Ahead, in the wide valley,

Lee could see the small river, running fairly well under what looked to be a still-standing concrete bridge.

They would have water shortly.

"What are you confused about?" Lee asked.

"Why did he take you three hundred years into your future?"

Lee nodded. "When you are in another timeline, only two minutes and fifteen seconds pass in the timeline you are in."

"No matter how long you stay in the other timeline?" Joan asked.

"No matter how long," Lee said. "In your original timeline, you just age a few minutes, even if you lived and died a full life in the other timeline."

"That's why you said that if you had died in the horse accident, you would have been fine."

Lee nodded.

"Still not understanding the reason for moving you into the future," Joan said.

"I was taken there to set my time," he said. "I jumped back one hundred years on my own. Then another hundred, and then another hundred, ending back up in my original time. So if I was killed in my original time, say in 2018, I would end up a hundred years in the future with only two minutes having passed. And I could go back into another timeline and keep living."

"Oh," she said. Then she whispered, "You're immortal, for all intents and purposes."

"I am," Lee said, feeling a little odd that she had put it that way. "Never think about it like that, but yes. And now you will be as well, if we get out of this."

She stopped and just stared at him. He took a few steps before he realized she had stopped. He turned and she was just staring. He couldn't tell if she was angry or what.

"You want to explain that?"

"If we get out of this, it's going to be through the crystals at the institute."

"Yes," she said.

"That means we will both be jumping back from this timeline, so both of us will ultimately be based here. And with each hundred-year jump back in time, we will be set in each new timeline."

"So that means if we get back and I live a full life and die in old age in my original time, I will end up back here, young again.

"No, you will end up one hundred years in the future, young again. Every time we jump backwards, that becomes the point we return to with only two minutes having passed. If this really is 2728 and we can get the crystals to work, we will have seven jumps between our time and here."

"Immortal," she said softly.

"If first we can not die getting to the institute, if the institute is still there, and if we can get the crystals to work," Lee said. "Three very large ifs."

Joan nodded and started walking again.

They turned toward the river ahead of them.

Now he was even more impressed by her. He understood the math, understood timelines, and he had still been shocked to his core when he realized he would be immortal, able to live as many lifetimes as he wanted to live.

His problem now was that he wasn't sure that if he died here, he would end up back in any timeline. He was in the future, ahead of any point he was set.

Joan hadn't gone into a crystal. He was pretty sure that if she died, she would be forever dead. This was just the future of her normal timeline.

And he wasn't going to let her die if he had anything to say about it.

SIXTEEN

September 7th, 2728
Old Highway 45, Southern Idaho

JOAN AND LEE GOT The glass bottles they were carrying for water washed out completely and then filled.

They both took long drinks of the crystal clear and cold water and sat in the shade of a nearby tree while they ate a decent number of pine nuts. It was amazing how filling the pine nuts were when combined with water.

By the time they finished their lunch, it was almost one in the afternoon and she felt refreshed and ready to go.

Since Joan and Steph usually had lunch together, this was the first time since all this happened that Joan wondered how Steph was doing. It must have been horrid for her to see her best friend just vanish.

Joan missed Steph and Joan wanted more than anything else to have the chance to just go back with Steph and curl up and tell her all about this nightmare over drinks.

Maybe that might happen.

Looking around at the dead world, Joan doubted it.

She looked at the handsome man sitting beside her. If there was any hope of them surviving and her getting to tell

Steph everything, it would be up to Lee. Joan would help where she could, but he was the one who really understood all this.

They set off again, first climbing out of the small valley and then after a few more miles seeming to hit slightly rolling farmland.

Farmhouses sat back off the road and all looked completely abandoned. A couple had already fallen into piles of rubble.

After their talk about timelines, she had tried to push that out of her mind and just focus on the task at hand, and that was making it to Boise and the institute there alive.

They had enough pine nuts for a decent dinner and then maybe some tomorrow morning, but after that they would be going hungry again if they didn't find some sort of food.

She was just about to ask Lee if he had any ideas about that when they crested over a hill and he pointed out ahead. "That's the south side of Nampa."

Nampa was a decent-sized town close to Boise and now she was back where she knew the area.

Or actually, she had known the area seven hundred years in the past. At least she knew the name of the town, and that made her feel a little better.

Now as they worked their way along the crumbling highway, they started passing small subdivisions. Some of the homes were very futuristic modern-looking and all were slowly being reclaimed by nature.

"I wonder if malls still existed before all this happened," Lee said.

"I got a hunch we're going to find out shortly," she said. "Why?"

He pointed to his feet. One of the boots was starting to come apart at a seam.

"I could use finding a shoe store."

She stopped him and took another strip of cloth from the bottom of her now much-shorter smock and wrapped it tightly around the boot to give it support.

"Thanks," he said. "That should get me the next few miles and into Nampa just fine."

It did, but barely. They had to stop twice more to give the boots more support. Clearly anything leather or cloth wasn't going to have much lifespan. They needed to find shoes that were all synthetic and rubber to have any chance of wear. And she wasn't so sure about the rubber parts. Over one hundred years was a very long time.

It was after five in the evening when they finally reached what she remembered to be a large mall area on the Boise side of Nampa. Nothing looked the same, including the overhead monorail tracks, the modern sweeping roads, or the buildings, some of which climbed a dozen stories into the air.

In her time Nampa was a farming and bedroom town. She doubted it had had any building over a few stories tall back then.

And it was just outside of Nampa that they had found their first stopped car. Or at least Joan thought it was a car. More like a sleek-lined mini-bus. It had a mummified skeleton in the back seat dressed in what looked like a dark suit and no steering wheel or driver.

The car must have had some feature that had caused it to stop right in the middle of the road. A tree was growing up against it now.

"Driverless cars were a norm in 2318," Lee said. "Never seen anything like this one before, but clearly driverless."

She looked at Lee, feeling stunned again. "Driverless cars? How?"

He glanced at her, then laughed. "You think that's something, wait until I show you a phone just from my time. He moved over to the car and looked at the mummified body inside. "See the thin band on his wrist?"

She looked at what he was pointing to. It seemed like nothing more than a thin rubber band.

"More than likely his phone, computer, and connection to the car," Lee said. "And who knows what else. My guess is that when everyone was killed, this society was very advanced. More than either one of us can even imagine."

"So we're looking at things and thinking they are something similar to something from our own time," Joan said. "Like this car or whatever it is."

"Chances are people of this time didn't even have personal transportation and just had public vehicles that took them where they needed to go if it was outside a normal mass-transit area."

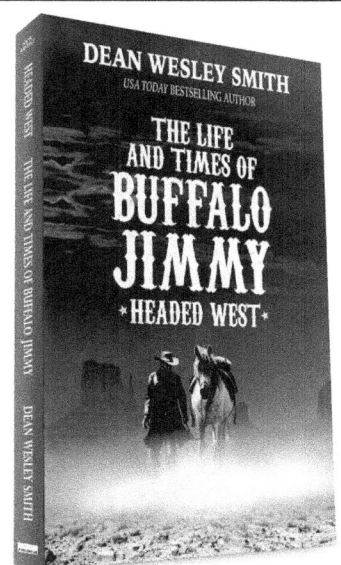

Now Available
**from all your favorite booksellers
in trade paper and electronic editions.**

"Was that the way it was headed in 2318?" Joan asked.

"Honestly don't know," Lee said, shrugging as they kept walking. "I was more interested in spending time in the past on my ranch in central Idaho studying time itself rather than figuring out what humans were doing with all the time."

"Didn't much like people, huh?"

"Not much," he said. "Present company excepted."

"Thank you," she said, smiling at him.

He smiled as well and they just kept on walking.

She was really enjoying spending time with this handsome and very smart man. She just hoped they could survive this and continue to spend time together.

Even if it was only walking in silence.

SEVENTEEN

September 7th, 2728
Outside Nampa, Idaho

LEE WAS HAPPY when they managed to get through the dead city of Nampa and to the Boise side. In front of them was clearly a massive center full of stores. So malls had survived, at least in one form or another. He had a hunch they might, since gathering places for people to shop and exchange things had been part of society for thousands of years ahead of his time. It would make sense that gathering places would continue forward.

As they had worked their way through the town, they had seen human remains everywhere, sometimes in vehicles, sometimes slumped in restaurants beside the streets.

Whatever had killed everyone had been sudden, of that there was no doubt. No one looked to have been running to get away from anything. They all just died instantly.

And along the edges of the streets were thousands of small white bones. It was Joan who figured out they were bird bones.

The sun was low on the horizon and Lee had no doubt they needed to find a place to stay for the night. And he was going to need to find some sort of shoes for the twenty-mile hike into Boise from where they were. The boots he had borrowed were just about finished. Right now only parts of Joan's lab coat were even holding one of them together at all.

The huge mall they had found was like walking into a massive sports stadium. There were maybe six or seven levels of stores and what looked like restaurants as far as they could see.

A couple areas looked to be filled with entertainment of some sort. He couldn't make any sense of it, so he didn't try.

"This place could hold thousands of people and not seem crowded," Joan said, her voice hushed.

Lee just stared in awe of the modern lines of the sweeping architecture and how everything seemed welcoming and pleasing, even after sitting dead for more than a hundred years.

Wide sidewalks that looked like they had once moved weaved through the place. Massive trees had grown up in the center and surprisingly, the roof and much of the structure still looked solid.

Even the layer of dust that seemed to cover everything manmade wasn't as bad in here.

There were only a few human remains that they could see, and they had on a form of green uniform. Either security or janitorial staff, from the looks of them.

As he and Joan stepped into the large area, looking around in the gloom, lights came on.

Many of the lights weren't working, but enough were to make the place much nicer than the gloom of evening.

"How is that possible?" Joan asked, looking around.

"Solar power, entire building not on a power grid," Lee said. "Duster had the institute set up off the grid as well. So this is encouraging for having the institute power work."

"That normal in the future?" she asked.

"I think it would be," he said. "Different forms of energy were common even in my time."

She nodded, then pointed at a store on the second level. "First things first, we get you shoes."

"That sounds like a wonderful idea and my feet and legs will thank you," he said.

The shoe store she had seen was huge and as they entered, lights came up and a soft background music he didn't recognize started to play.

"Now that's creepy," she said, looking around.

And it was creepy.

But it didn't stop him from finding some synthetic tennis shoes, or at least they looked like a tennis or jogging shoe. They felt wonderful on his feet and they didn't seem to want to come apart any time soon.

He found a second pair and put them in his backpack.

Joan found a second pair as well and replaced the woman's shoes she had found with a new pair.

"Now we need camping supplies," he said as they left the store.

A woman's voice came out of the air around them. "Camping supplies for various outdoor activities can be found in two locations."

The voice went on to give them directions to both stores and a holographic image of their path through the mall to the stores appeared in front of them.

Joan said simply, "Thank you."

"You are more than welcome," the voice said.

She looked at him with wide eyes and he just laughed. It was great to see Joan, the woman who had seemed like a rock so far, shocked by a computer voice out of the past.

It made her even more attractive to him. More human.

EIGHTEEN

September 7th, 2728
Outside Nampa, Idaho

JOAN FELT ALMOST comfortable in the huge, empty futuristic mall. They had found the camping equipment store thanks to some woman's voice that Lee called a computer voice. In the camping store, Lee wanted things to filter water and take bacteria out of water. They both put pills and small water filters in their packs.

Then Lee went over to what had been the camping food area. Aisle after aisle of packages and containers.

Joan was surprised that he was even thinking of that after a hundred years, but as he started looking through the packages, he started laughing.

"Good until 2820," he said, handing her a freeze-dried packet of beef stew.

"Still good for almost another hundred years," she said, shaking her head in amazement. "But you actually think they would be safe to eat?"

"I am assuming a great deal for 2600s technology," he said. "But better that we have something to try when the pine nuts run out."

She only nodded to that. Eating food prepared over a hundred years before didn't really give her confidence, but Lee seemed to think that most of it would be fine.

They both added three double meals to their small backpacks and then found small, light pans and a few cups and travel silverware. If they were good enough to eat, Lee figured that there would be stores like this one in Boise they could raid. No point in carrying extra. Or if they had to, they could always come back.

Now Available
**from all your favorite booksellers
in trade paper and electronic editions.**

"No surprise that camping gear hasn't changed much in all the centuries," Lee said. "Just got way lighter."

She had to agree with that. Even with an extra pair of shoes in her pack, it was still very, very light.

"Changes of clothes and then someplace to sleep," Lee said as they headed out of the store.

It turned out that most of the clothing they found just fell apart on touch. They finally ended up with an extra pair of synthetic fiber pants each and a couple shirts each that seemed like they might hold together.

And they found underwear and socks.

"After the long day walking it would be nice to have a hot springs around here," she said.

"Yeah, that would be nice," Lee said. "Can't imagine the water would be working, though."

She shrugged and pointed to a woman's restroom. "I need to pee, so think I'll go find out."

"Good idea," he said and headed for the men's room.

The restroom was huge and seemed to have small rooms for toilets instead of stalls. And actually, the rooms weren't so small either with sliding doors that went back into the walls.

She put her pack on the counter and went into one of the small rooms. The light came up as she entered. Water still filled the toilet basin and it didn't look like it had been sitting there very long at all.

She started to slide the door closed, then changed her mind and left it halfway open. No point in taking a chance of being trapped in a toilet stall.

When she was finished, she stood up to try to figure out how to flush the toilet, but there were no handles.

As she slid the door back completely open, the toilet flushed behind her, making her spin around and watch the water go down the drain and then the basin fill back up.

She just stood there and watched, stunned. The water looked clean and clear. No sign of sitting in pipes for a century.

She tried the sink, but there were no handles on the faucets and she couldn't get water to run at all, so she grabbed her pack and went back into the mall.

Lee looked like he had washed his face and poured water over his head.

"The water is working," he said, smiling.

"Couldn't get the sink to work in there," she said.

"Put your hand under where the water comes out," Lee said.

She shook her head, dropped her pack, and went back into the bathroom. The moment she put her hand under what seemed to be the faucet, water ran out, clear and clean and with a strong current.

She washed her face, her neck and dampened her hair to get what dirt she could off of it. The water smelled pure and clean. Amazing, just amazing.

She went back out to where Lee was sitting, smiling.

"How is that possible?" she asked.

"I'm guessing well water for the entire facility," Lee said, "electrical self-contained for just the mall, more than likely solar. Toilets flushing and sinks running automatically at regular times so the water kept moving through everything over all the years. Won't last forever, but clearly has lasted for over a hundred years now."

She felt a sense of relief. "Looks like we have a place here to retreat to if we can't get back to our time through the institute."

Lee nodded, looking around at the massive mall. "Better than dying of thirst or starving, that's for sure."

"So we need a furniture and bedding store next," she said.

Again a woman's voice right in front of her surprised Joan.

The woman told Joan how to find one of three furniture stores in the mall and a map appeared in front of Joan's face.

"Thank you," Joan said once again.

"You are welcome," the voice said.

Joan just looked at Lee, who was laughing lightly. More than likely the look on her face told him how she really felt about the voice. It bothered her a lot.

Creepy, just damn creepy.

NINETEEN

September 8th, 2728
Outside Nampa, Idaho

LEE AND JOAN had slept on real beds in a bedding store. They hadn't slept in the same bed, but in beds side-by-side. And for Lee, it had felt heavenly. For some reason, the beds of the future just felt like they didn't allow a pressure point anywhere.

He couldn't remember the last time he had slept that soundly.

He woke up before Joan and lay there and stared at her. She was on her back, one arm above her head, her hair spread out over the pillow. She was beautiful, of that there was no doubt. And smart and fun to be with, even when they faced death and never getting home again.

He had never imagined a woman like her. And he didn't much like that he was starting to fall for her, but he wasn't going to fight it.

He had no idea if she liked him, but at the moment, that didn't matter. At the moment it was pretty clear they were the last two people left alive on the planet. Lee and Joan, a very strange Adam and Eve, that was for sure.

Finally, his bladder forced him to get up and that caused Joan to open her eyes look around at the high ceilings of the furniture store and then at him.

"Damn, it wasn't a dream," she said. "I keep hoping this is all a dream."

Before going to sleep, he had taken off his pants and shirt, sleeping only in his underwear.

So as he pulled on his pants, Joan crawled out of bed, yawned, and came around to his bed. She was wearing only a bra and panties and looked wonderful.

"Let me check those feet," she said. "Before you put on shoes."

They had found some sort of medicine in a back room of the furniture store and Joan knew the medical names of much of it, so she used some antibiotic cream on the sores and blisters of his feet.

This morning she did the same, then helped him into a fresh pair of socks.

"Your feet are looking better," she said, standing and stretching.

She clearly didn't mind at all letting him see her naked or half-naked. He liked that about her and he sure enjoyed the view.

He waited for her to get dressed, then they both headed for the bathrooms just outside the furniture store.

They both refilled glass bottles with fresh water. To be safe, he put a disinfectant pill in each bottle. The last thing they needed was to get a stomach virus of some sort. In these conditions, that could be deadly.

As they started for the door to the mall that they had come in, Joan said, "I wonder if the mall has an employee area with showers and a kitchen that might work."

Lee glanced at her. He was surprised he hadn't thought of that. If there was a kitchen, they might be able to boil some water and try one of the packaged meals. Better than another meal of just pine nuts.

"Mall," he said into the air, "would you please tell me where the employee entrance is to locker rooms and showers and break rooms?"

"The closest break room to your location is to your right just ahead," the woman's voice said.

"Please open the door for us," Lee said.

A door that couldn't be seen in the wall clicked and swung open.

"Thank you," Joan said.

The woman's voice said, "You are welcome."

It took them ten minutes of walking behind the scenes in the wide employee and shipping hallways before they found what looked to be a kitchen in a break room.

They heated up some water to a boil and tried a beef stew package.

It was stunningly good.

"This tastes as good as you could get in a restaurant," Joan said, shaking her head.

"Well," Lee said, smiling at her and agreeing completely. "At least the camping food improved over the centuries."

TWENTY

September 8th, 2728
Boise, Idaho

JOAN FIGURED A twenty-mile walk was going to be difficult for them in one day, but Lee thought they could manage it if they paced themselves and took regular breaks.

And they were getting an early start, since by the time they left the future mall, the sun was just starting to color the mountains around the large valley. Joan felt refreshed and actually full. That stew had tasted amazing and they had put what they couldn't eat in a glass jar for lunch.

Luckily for them, the day turned out to be cool and overcast, but it never rained. So the temperatures were comfortable and didn't drain them.

Around her almost nothing looked the same as her time. The valley had clearly filled up with millions more people than in her time and gone upward in many places with buildings. She couldn't even begin to count the numbers of towering skyscrapers that dotted the path ahead.

As they passed one forty-story building, Lee pointed at it. "Farming went vertical," he said.

He was right. Every floor looked to be filled with massive plants, clearly overgrown because of time.

The future looked to have been an interesting place if everyone hadn't died suddenly.

The roads here were in as bad of shape as the ones in the county, and there were a lot more stopped cars with the remains of a human slumped in the back.

There had also been some sort of very futuristic-looking metal tube that was a train of some sort that was elevated in many places along the way. All the glass cars that ran along the tube were stopped and almost all of them were full of dead humans, mostly mummified.

At first she looked at them all, in every car, but after a while she made herself stop. The realization that they were all people who had lost their lives finally outweighed her normal doctor curiosity.

Lee just didn't look at any of them at all, instead keeping his gaze ahead to pick out their path through the destruction Mother Nature was doing on a once thriving civilization.

When he wanted to, he clearly had the ability to focus. And it seemed his focus was on their survival and getting them home. She didn't mind that at all.

They stopped for a rest every hour and by the middle of the afternoon they were almost to where her building had been to the west of downtown Boise.

But as they walked along what had been a very wide road, she could tell her building was gone. Completely gone and in its place was a massive skyscraper that towered a good eighty stories in the air.

She decided to take Lee's approach and not look as they walked past it. Her entire life's work had been in her building, in her patients. Now they were all almost seven hundred years dead.

By three in the afternoon they reached the far side of Boise and stopped for a meal.

"Only a few more miles," Lee said.

He started a small fire in the middle of the road using kindling from a crumbling building nearby, then heated up some of their water and mixed up a pack of a chicken dish.

It actually smelled and tasted wonderful, again as good as something she might order in a restaurant.

They both sat, eating slowly. In the twenty miles they had barely talked and honestly she hadn't minded. She liked being alone with her thoughts normally and clearly Lee did as well.

But sitting on the old curb near downtown Boise, she had to ask Lee a question that had been bothering her.

"If Duster and Bonnie and your friends know all about time and can travel at will back in time," Joan said, "how come your friends didn't just go back and stop you from falling off the horse when they figured out you were missing?"

"That we were missing," Lee said. "They would go back and watch exactly what happened. My guess is that one of the nurses waiting on me in your center was from the future. Guy by the name of Craig?"

"I knew Craig for ten years," Joan said, looking at Lee with a frown.

"Remember, ten years is just over two minutes in Craig's real time."

"Oh," Joan said. She couldn't get her mind around someone coming back from the future and working for a decade or more to just be in a position to find out what happened.

"So if Craig was a traveler, why didn't he stop us from jumping here?"

Lee shrugged. "Duster told them to just go find out what happened, more than likely."

"So if you and I go missing and they know how it happened," Joan said, now more puzzled than ever, "I still don't understand why didn't they just stop it?"

"More than likely in an infinite number of timelines they did," Lee said.

She stopped eating and just stared at him.

"There are always two sides to any decision," Lee said. "If Duster and Bonnie decided to stop us from vanishing and me falling off that horse, there are still an infinite number of timelines that they decided not to."

"And we're in one of those?" Joan asked.

Lee just shrugged and kept eating. "No way of knowing if they even tried. We are here, this is our timeline, we play the cards dealt in this game."

"But why wouldn't they try?" Joan asked.

"Because if they did try, they would fail for an infinite number of us," Lee said. "There is no way in time to make a decision without both sides happening."

"But no decision is a decision," she said.

He nodded. "It is the moment you make the decision to make no decision. Yes."

"So in an infinite number of universes, we don't meet, and an infinite number we end up here."

"Maybe," Lee said. "Time is interesting in that if a timeline makes no difference, it will fold back into the timeline it separated from."

"I have no idea how that will apply to us," she said.

Lee shrugged and then smiled at her. "As the old saying goes, only time will tell."

"You know," she said, "this time travel stuff can give a person a headache."

"I've heard a lot of people say that," Lee said, still smiling at her.

She just shook her head and went back to trying to finish her wonderful chicken dinner.

Around them the dead city of Boise made no noise at all.

PART FOUR
Decisions

TWENTY-ONE

August 7th, 2018
Central, Idaho

DUSTER AND BONNIE and Parks and Dawn sat talking quietly about the possibilities of what might happen as they ate dinner.

The wonderful pine rafters and log walls around them kept the sound down, and the smells from their dinners filled the air.

Duster's steak was melt-in-his-mouth good, as always, but he barely noticed it. And the sautéed mushrooms and baked potato on his plate were mostly untouched. What they were facing was just too impossible to try to deal with. He ate the steak, but that was all he was going to get down.

And they still needed more information.

He didn't want to lose his friend Lee, but there might not be a choice. Or if they made a choice to save him before they jumped, Lee and Dr. Failor still would be lost in an infinite number of timelines where nothing was done to save them.

Impossible decision. There had to be a way to save them in all timelines, but the solution just wasn't coming to him or Bonnie or anyone else for that matter.

Just as he was finishing the last bit of his steak, his phone rang and he picked it up from where he had left it in front of his plate and said, "Yes."

"Our best calculations," Brice said, "is that they ended up about thirty caverns deep."

"And what will that mean?" Duster said.

"If they picked the right direction and started walking at a decent pace and thirst and hunger didn't get them, they would get into the last cavern about a hundred-and-ten to a hundred-and-fifty years after the event, depending on how fast they walked. It's a very long distance and Lee would be barefoot because he was in a hospital bed."

Duster just shook his head and looked at the worried expressions on his friends around him. It was bad enough that they were in the caverns, but when they came out, they would find a world destroyed by an intense emission from an exploding star. The entire solar system took a full hit and the event killed all human, animal, fish, and insect life of the planet instantly, without warning. And it had killed all the humans on the moon and on Mars and mining the asteroids. Only plants remained that didn't depend on insect and birds. Lower level bacteria also survived.

Duster couldn't even imagine seeing that world.

"Has Lee ever been to the cavern?" Brice asked.

"No," Duster said. "Thanks, Brice. If you and Dixie come up with anything more, call me. But take no action unless we say."

"Understood," Brice said. "We'll keep working on it until we find a solution."

Duster put the phone down and looked at Bonnie. He hadn't seen such a worried expression on her beautiful face in centuries. If ever.

"If they can get out of the caverns," Duster said, "and if the airlock doors still work to the mine tunnel, and if they don't die of thirst first, they are well over a hundred years after the event."

"Oh, no," Parks said.

All of them understood the dead world Lee and Dr. Failor would find themselves in.

"How far can we jump after the event?" Dawn asked.

"Seven years," Park said. "That's all the time that has passed in regular time since we discovered the event and saved our people."

Silence filled the room.

Duster knew that Lee was tough, and he knew that Dr. Failor was smart from the reports he had read when they decided to fund her work. Maybe together they could get to the institute somehow.

But even if they did, Duster had no idea what Lee would do. Lee and Dr. Failor would be just too far into the future.

The crystals that were there after the event would only jump them back a hundred years, if the boxes still worked. Duster was certain the boxes would work, but the boxes would limit how far they could come.

In other words, Lee and Dr. Failor were trapped after the event. And there was no way anyone could get to them.

Or even send a message into the future to them.

TWENTY-TWO

September 8th, 2728
Boise, Idaho

LEE AND JOAN made the institute on Warm Springs Avenue by five in the evening, with less than an hour of daylight left. In the camping shop, Lee had picked up a couple small lanterns that burned a paraffin fuel, but he hoped they didn't have to use them.

"Wow, looks like it hasn't changed at all," Joan said, staring at the Victorian mansion tucked among massive old oak and willow trees.

Lee could see lots of weeds and places the old building needed a lot of work, but she was right, the building looked almost identical to how it had looked when Duster and Bonnie and a few others built it in 1880.

Considering all the crumbling modern architecture they had been walking through, it felt like a familiar friend welcoming him home.

They went up on the wide wooden porch, moving carefully to make sure no boards had rotted out, and then to the massive wooden front door.

"Locked or unlocked?" Joan asked.

"Unlocked," Lee said. "The disaster that killed everyone came with no warning. And besides, no one ever locked this door."

She nodded and he tested the door, pushing it open on hinges that squealed.

Lights came up as they entered and he sighed with relief.

"That's a good sign, right?" Joan asked.

"A very good sign," Lee said. "If there's power, we can hope there's going to be fresh water as well, just as with the mall. This complex is completely self-contained and has been from day one."

"This place looks like it was frozen in 1880," Joan said, looking around at the long drapes, the period couches, the old desk, everything.

"Historical institute," he said. "Part of the charm and the cover."

Lee went to where he knew a hidden doorway was and pushed on a latch and the door slid open in the wood panel.

"That's nifty," Joan said, following him into the hallway beyond.

It hadn't changed either, as far as Lee could tell.

He went to the staircase and led Joan downward.

Lights came on as they descended and turned off behind them.

Finally, at the bottom, he pulled on a large door, holding his breath that it would open.

It did and he stepped into what everyone in his time called the living room.

The lights came up and behind him Joan said, "Wow."

The room was a large cavern with a kitchen against the black lava rock on one wall, bathrooms off to one side, many, many couches and chairs, and a massive stone fireplace filling the middle.

Doors and corridors led off of the big space in all directions.

The furniture was still in place and the kitchen counter looked solid.

He had spent many an hour sitting at that counter talking with Bonnie and Duster.

He moved over and put his pack on the counter, then stood and looked around. It seemed the same, yet very modern. Some of the couches and chairs were clearly from the time of the disaster, while others were from previous time periods.

"This is really amazing," Joan said. "But what I find encouraging is that there are no bodies here."

Now Available
from all your favorite booksellers
in trade paper and electronic editions.

Lee sort of jerked and looked around. She was right, no bodies.

He took a deep breath and tried to let himself think.

"Is it encouraging?" Joan asked.

"I think it might be," Lee said, nodding. "It means they jumped in here after the disaster that killed everyone. So time is still going forward for those crystals that might be able to get us back to a time before the disaster."

But he had a hunch it wasn't going to work that way.

TWENTY-THREE

September 8th, 2728
Boise, Idaho

JOAN COULDN'T BELIEVE the massive cavern that was under the old Victorian home. She had driven along Warm Springs Avenue many times and past this building and always marveled at how amazing it looked.

But now, being under it and knowing this cave had been under it in her time just shocked her.

"So what do we do now?" Joan asked Lee, who was standing at the counter, clearly lost in thought.

"We need to explore," he said, nodding to her.

He led her in the direction across the cavern toward a door to the back left of the big cave and then down two flights of stone stairs.

She was very relieved when the lights in the stairways came on as they descended.

This could have easily been one of those closed-in dark places she hated so much.

"So do you know where we are heading?"

Lee nodded and opened a door at the bottom of the stairs to show beyond a large, empty cavern.

Joan was again shocked. This entire complex must have stretched for a long way along Warm Springs Avenue. How could the city not know about it?

"This was where all the supplies were kept for those traveling back into the Old West, meaning Boise from 1890 onward. You got dressed here for the time period you were heading to."

She nodded, looking around at the massive cavern. This could have held more clothes and supplies than five department stores.

He went across the big room with her following. A long wall of doors stood open on the other side. He looked in the first door and shook his head, clearly not happy with what he saw.

She could see that the room was carved out of solid stone and was long and very narrow, with wire fence running down both sides. There were spots in the rock walls behind the wire fence carved out.

"Let me guess," she said, "the crystals were in those places in the walls."

Lee nodded.

He moved over a door and looked in, again shaking his head. "The crystal I used to go back the last time had been in here."

"That's the one I am from?" she asked.

He shrugged. "You and I are from every crystal that had been in all these rooms. Every timeline was so identical, it was impossible to tell them apart. But yes, a crystal in this room was my gateway to that timeline and the events in that timeline happened to me and you in every crystal at the same time."

She let that sink in for a moment as she stared down the long, narrow cave at the hundreds, maybe thousands of niches in the rock walls.

"As I said before, thinking about timelines really can give a person a headache," she said.

He just laughed softly.

"So why do they take the crystals away?" Joan asked.

"The institute functions as a sort of way station," Lee said. "Except for the crystals that had been in here, a traveler from any time can only go back a maximum of one hundred years. Then they have to change rooms to keep going back, if they have permission."

"Like changing trains," Joan said.

Lee nodded. "A failsafe that Duster and Bonnie put into every device when they set up this institute."

"So we need to find where the last crystals are and jump back a hundred years," she said, surprised that those words had even come out of her mouth.

Lee nodded, but didn't look happy. "I'm betting the disaster that killed everyone was more than a hundred years ago. That means those crystals have been sitting here for that long and no new ones put in because no one could get very far past the disaster."

Joan stared at him where he stood thinking.

If that was the case, they could jump back a hundred years and still be trapped here, after the time the world was destroyed.

She didn't want to panic, but for the first time since being in that mine tunnel, she was starting to feel that way.

Lee finally nodded to himself. "Let's go see if we can find the crystals," he said. "At least that will be a start. I just hope Duster and Parks didn't come in after the disaster and remove them all."

"Why would they do that?" Joan asked, turning to follow Lee back across the empty cavern toward the door.

"More than likely they wouldn't," Lee said. "But when you can spend an eternity in the past with live people, not much reason to come to the world we just walked through."

She had to admit that he had a point there.

TWENTY-FOUR

September 8th, 2728
Boise, Idaho

LEE AND JOAN explored empty cavern after empty cavern, climbing up and down stone stairs for almost an hour before Joan said they needed a break. Lee wanted to keep going, but his feet were hurting and he knew she was right.

They went back to the kitchen area of the big cavern and both of them used the rest rooms, which still had water flowing, same as the big mall.

Lee then tried the stove behind the counter and was surprised that it actually worked. He boiled some water and cooked another of the beef stew camping meals. They sat at the counter drinking water and eating stew.

He had no idea if they could find the crystals, if there still were crystals here, or if the wooden boxes that Bonnie and Duster had built that allowed someone to step into the past of a timeline would still work.

And if it did work, would the limit of one hundred years still hold them to a place after the disaster that killed everything and everyone?

About halfway through their meal, Joan asked, "You didn't know about the disaster. Do you think Bonnie and Duster did?"

"I think so," Lee said. "I always found it odd that he never talked about the institute moving forward past the year 2318. I never asked, but sort of guessed that something happened in the next hundred years."

"But it looks like this disaster happened in just over a hundred years ago," Joan said, "not four hundred years ago."

"I agree," Lee said. "But from the looks of how modern all this is around here, how it fits with the world, they clearly made it up to the disaster."

"And they had to come in here after and clear out the bodies of those who died," Joan said.

Lee shook his head and glanced at the beautiful woman sitting beside him. "Wouldn't work that way. Lots of them might have died, but the moment someone unplugged a crystal and came back after the disaster, they would go back and save everyone from even dying in the first place. Since that would be what would happen in every timeline because there would be no decision to not do that, no one would actually be killed here."

She shook her head. "Headache again."

He laughed. "You are actually grasping this better than most ever would."

"Thank you," she said, smiling at him. "But not sure that means much."

"It actually helps a lot," he said.

They finished up their meals, put their dishes in the sink, and then headed back in search.

It was on the third flight of stairs after lunch they had gone down that they found the cavern that still had supplies in it. Tables of stuff, seemingly miles of clothing. Of course, all the supplies were well over a hundred years old, most of the clothing rotted and useless, but it made Lee clap his hands in excitement.

"I don't recognize much of any of this stuff," she said. "I feel like someone from the fifteen hundreds looking at a department store from nineteen eighty-five."

He had to agree with her. That's exactly what it felt like. Most of stuff and a lot of the clothes looked odd and a bunch of things he flat didn't recognize or could even figure out what they were used for.

He led the way through the cavern and to the first door with crystals and opened it.

It was a heavenly sight.

A thousand crystals glowed along both walls and wooden tables sat in the middle of the long cavern.

Wires ran from boxes on the tables toward an area of crystals on the other side of the wire fence.

"Oh, my," she said as she stood beside him in the door.

He walked over and touched the first wooden box. It seemed solid enough. And the wires seemed flexible enough. The devices might still be working.

He turned and smiled. "Let's go get our packs and see if we can catch a train out of here."

"Wow, does that sound wonderful."

He had to agree. It did.

It really did.

TWENTY-FIVE

September 8th, 2628
Boise, Idaho

JOAN HAD HERSELF scared to death by the time they got their packs and made it back down to the crystal room.

"What is this going to feel like?" she asked Lee as he picked up a pair of gloves and went through the wire cage and hooked ends of the wires to wires around the crystal.

"Did you feel anything when we jumped into the cavern?" Lee asked as he came out of the cage and hooked a black wire to a black terminal on one of the boxes.

"Not a thing," she said.

"That's what it feels like," he said. "Nothing, no movement, no time in transit, nothing."

She nodded.

She watched as he set a timer on the box for September 8th, 2628, one hundred years in the past from where they stood.

Then he hooked up the other wire and took off the gloves.

"Got your pack on your back securely?" he asked, checking his pack as he asked.

She checked her pack and nodded. "Got it."

"Now when I say so, touch the wooden box with one bare hand at the same moment I do," he said.

She nodded. There was no chance she could even speak. Regular terror moments seemed to be a part of this entire thing.

"Three, two, one, now," Lee said.

They both touched the wooden box at the same moment.

"Nothing happened," she said as they both stepped back.

The room was exactly the same as a moment before.

"We should be one hundred years closer to home," he said. "And if we need to go back to that time, we just unhook those wires."

She looked at the two wires still hooked up and nodded.

He turned and led the way out of the crystal room and into the supply room.

It was clear at a glance they had made it. Same clothes and stuff sat on the tables, but now it all looked new and wasn't covered with much dust at all.

They quickly made their way through all the supplies and headed back up the stone staircase toward the main room. She was feeling excited. Were they really going to get home?

Was this nightmare about to be over?

The large main room looked almost the same as when they left it. The only difference was that when the lights came up as they entered, they were brighter because fewer bulbs had burnt out.

But all the furniture was the same and there was no one around.

Lee put his pack on the counter and turned to her. "We didn't make it back past the disaster," Lee said.

"Damn."

Lee nodded and looked around. "We need to go upstairs and outside to try to figure out exactly when the disaster happened."

She nodded and followed him to an elevator.

"You think it's safe?" she asked.

"I'm sure it is now, but I sure wouldn't have tried it a hundred years from now."

She nodded to that and a moment after the doors closed they opened again to show the same hidden room they had come in through. Smoothest and fastest elevator she had ever been on.

Lee opened the secret panel and went back out into the front room that looked like they had stepped back into 1890, then toward the big wooden front door.

Outside, the evening air had a bite to it and everything was deadly silent. Not even a wind rustled the leaves in the oak trees around them.

The lights of the mansion were the only lights in the entire town that she could see.

Lee went down the sidewalk and out the front gate of the institute, heading toward one of the driverless cars. Lee stayed right with him.

In the back seat of the strange-looking mini-bus-like car, a person sat, clearly dead.

She took one look at the body in the sealed car and just shook her head.

"Got any idea how long ago this person died?"

She nodded. "At least twenty years ago."

Lee just stood there, saying nothing as behind them the lights of the mansion blinked off, leaving them in darkness in the middle of a futuristic street next to a dead person.

"Now what do we do?" she asked softly.

He reached out and took her hand and they turned back toward the mansion. "I honestly don't know."

And that from the most brilliant man she had ever met scared her more than anything had so far.

PART FIVE
Impossible Choices

TWENTY-SIX

August 7th, 2018
Central, Idaho

DUSTER, BONNIE, DAWN, and Parks all just sat staring into space, thinking, as a waiter cleared off their dinner plates and brought them all coffee. Duster ignored the coffee and got a refill of iced tea instead.

His steak had been good, but he really hadn't enjoyed it.

After the waiter was gone, they still just sat there.

No one saying a word.

All of them were trying to figure out a way to save Lee and Dr. Failor, but Duster had no doubt that if they could be saved in all timelines, Lee and Dr. Failor had to do it themselves.

But even then, if they had made decisions along the way, then timelines split off where they didn't save themselves. But Duster hoped that Lee understood that and made pretty much all logical decisions, so the split timelines just merged back in.

If anyone knew time and timelines, it was Lee.

And since no one was alive after the event, it made no difference to a timeline if Lee and Dr. Failor lived or died after the event. All the timelines would merge back one way or another.

It only mattered if they didn't die and got back before the event somehow.

So it came down to Lee saving the two of them.

Bonnie glanced over at Duster. "You think Lee can figure out how to save himself and Dr. Failor?"

"Knowing what we know, could you?" Duster asked.

Bonnie smiled. "I think so. Could you?"

Duster nodded. "I would hope so. But one hundred plus years after the event, just getting to the institute is going to be major and a dangerous undertaking. That's the part that worries me."

"If they do get back here," Bonnie said, "doing it right worries me even more."

Duster nodded to that.

Parks and Dawn were both looking at Bonnie and Duster like they had lost a nut.

"What are you two talking about?" Dawn asked.

Duster smiled and said, "Let me call Brice and Dixie first to see if they have narrowed it down any farther on how far into the caverns they were sent."

He took out his phone and a moment later Brice answered. Without even saying hello, Brice said, "They were dumped between 120 and 130 years after the event. How fast they got moving and how fast they walked would make it closer to one hundred and twenty than one hundred and thirty."

"Thanks," Duster said. "Anything else?"

"Nothing," Brice said. "I'll call you if we find anything."

Duster hung up, knowing for a fact that those two brilliant minds would not be able to come up with any way to save Lee and Dr. Failor in all timelines.

"As we already know," Duster said to Dawn and Park and Bonnie, "they didn't get close to the event since they would have arrived back by now. Brice and Dixie think they are at least one hundred and twenty years past the event."

"Will the crystals in the cavern get them back a hundred years closer?" Park asked. "Will the boxes and wiring still work?"

"We designed them to last a lot longer than that," Bonnie said, nodding.

"So yes," Duster said, "they will work."

"So there is thirteen years between when we can go in after the event and where they are," Dawn said. "Might as well be a million years."

Duster nodded, trying not to smile. "That might as well be, you are right."

"But you think Lee still might be able to save them?" Parks asked.

"I am hoping he can," Duster said. "Depends on so many factors I'm afraid.

"We all are hoping," Bonnie said.

And with that the four of them went back to sitting in silence.

Waiting.

That was all they dared do.

Any decision at that point might be deadly to Lee and Dr. Failor. So they could make no decision, not even a decision to not decide.

TWENTY-SEVEN

September 9th, 2628
Boise, Idaho

LEE FELT BETTER the next morning.

He and Joan had walked hand-in-hand back into the institute. Then they had gone exploring in the old mansion, finding a large bedroom with what looked to be a modern and very comfortable large bed in it. It was on the second floor and to the back.

To one side was a small table in a window with chairs around it and a large empty closet.

Off of the bedroom was an actual working bathroom with a working shower with hot water. And in another direction was a small working kitchen. It was like a small apartment and they decided they would make it their base.

To Lee the apartment felt comfortable, more than likely because it still retained the charm of the 1890s Victorian home.

They went back down into the big cavern and got their packs off the kitchen counter there, then went back up to the apartment.

"I claim first in the shower," she said, smiling at him as she pulled off her clothes and tossed them on a chair and then walked naked into the bathroom.

"Don't take all the hot water," he said, admiring her wonderful body as she went. She was the most beautiful woman he had ever seen, of that there was no doubt.

And maybe one of the smartest as well.

He sat in a chair and eased off his shoes and socks. His feet were a mess, but nothing looked infected. He was damn lucky, that was for sure.

He was almost naked when Joan appeared, soaking wet in the door of the bathroom, steam pouring out around her.

She smiled at him. "The shower is huge and the water temperature perfect. Come soap up my back."

Then she turned and went back into the bathroom leaving a trail of water on the wood floor.

He instantly felt like he was back in college again. But this time it was with a woman he respected and really was falling for.

He quickly pulled off his underwear and joined her under the wonderful spray of a shower.

It was heavenly, just heavenly, and Joan looked amazing with the water running off her perfect skin.

He soaped her back and then she soaped his.

Finally, at one point, they ended up kissing, pressed together.

And the kiss was wonderful.

Just wonderful.

Perfect, actually.

He had never had a kiss like it.

They dried each other off and crawled into the bed, holding each other.

They made love slowly, then passionately, and then fell asleep in each other's arms.

The next morning she was in the shower again when he awoke. The sun was just lighting up the trees outside the apartment windows. By the time he crawled out of bed and got into the bathroom, she was done.

They talked as she dried off and then he got into the shower. They needed to find a grocery store that might have food still worth salvaging, if there was such a thing as a grocery store. At least they needed to find a camping store with more freeze-dried meals. They knew those existed at least.

"Why wouldn't there be a grocery store?" she had asked at one point.

"In my time lots of groceries were starting to be delivered on demand," he said. "No telling how it would be done in this time."

She had said nothing to that.

Since the clothes in the stores were only twenty years old instead of over a hundred, they also figured they could find some comfortable things to wear that wouldn't fall apart.

They sat at the table in their room looking out through the trees and the grounds around the mansion below. They were eating some prepackaged ham and eggs that tasted amazingly good.

"Sounds to me," she said, "that we are talking about settling in for a long haul here."

"I've got a few ideas I want to try," he said, "to get us back to 2018. But it might take me some time to figure it out, so we might as well be comfortable."

She nodded to that. "Just tell me what I can do to help."

"Honestly," he said, looking at her, "I doubt I would have made it this far without your help."

She laughed and shook her head. "That's just silly and you know it. But a very nice thing to say, I must admit."

"It's the truth," he said, looking into her wonderful green eyes.

She just shook her head and went back to eating, but he had no doubt at all it was the truth.

And no doubt at all that he was falling in love.

TWENTY-EIGHT

September 9th, 2628
Boise, Idaho

LEE HAD BEEN the most gentle and wonderful lover she had ever had. They had both taken their time until they no longer could stay slow.

And sleeping in his arms and waking up beside him had been amazing. Even though they were in deep trouble and she was in a place she never could have even dreamed about, being with Lee made her feel confident they might just get back to where they belonged.

It felt right and natural, even when they were just walking and not talking, which they seemed to do a lot. And she felt no need to fill the silence with chatter either. She just felt comfortable with him all the way around.

They walked about ten blocks to where they both remembered there had been a large business complex six hundred years before. They found one of the large sporting goods stores in a smaller version of the mall they had first found.

But except for the course of the river below the institute, nothing at all seemed the same in Boise. Nothing.

As far as she was concerned, she might have well been walking in a city in another country.

And the silence was almost unnerving. Only a slight breeze rustled the trees. Nothing else except the sound of their steps.

It felt like she was in a bad movie with the sound turned off. Cities were supposed to have noise in them. Never silence.

Never.

They loaded up large packs with freeze-dried meals of all sorts, then found some clothes in a few clothing stores and then headed back to the institute.

"I need to get something," he said when they returned to the apartment and tossed the packs in the small kitchen and the clothes on the bed.

"You need my help?" she asked.

"Just going down to the cavern with the crystals and get some tools. I'll bring it all back up here."

She worried about the two of them splitting up, but she just nodded and then she focused on trying to organize the food they had grabbed in the tiny kitchen.

He came back carrying a tool belt over one shoulder and one of the wooden boxes that had been in the crystal room.

He set it on the small table they had eaten breakfast at. With the light over the table and the light from the morning outside, the table was almost bright. A perfect place to work.

"What's your idea?" she asked.

"To my knowledge," Lee said, "no one but Bonnie and Duster know what is inside these boxes."

She came over and looked at the wooden box that she had paid little attention to in the cave. It was about the size of an old breadbox her grandmother had had sitting on a counter. It would have been completely square if one of its sides hadn't been slanted down. So it was a box on three sides, but had a small top and a large bottom and one side slanted.

It had two posts on one side for hooking up wires. One was a red post, the other a black post.

The angled side was polished wood that sort of angled upward like you could put a book on it to read. That was where she and Lee had put their hands. On the narrow top was a date timer of sorts that was now just black, no date or time showing, but when they had jumped to this point, the timer had read a date clearly.

Lee picked the box up and said, "It's surprisingly light. And the wood looks just like a standard oak, polished and stained."

He turned it over and over in his hands.

"There's no way to get into it," she said.

Lee was frowning. "They had to put it together somehow."

With that he set the box down on the floor and took out a hammer.

"You think it will be safe to just break into it?"

Lee shrugged. "I honestly don't know, but I also don't see much choice and since we have thousands of these down in those caverns, sacrificing one or two to learn how they work seems to be worth the price."

"Before you just hit it with a hammer," she said, reaching down and picking up the light wooden box, "let's try a few other tricks."

"Like what?" he asked, putting the hammer back on the tool belt.

"Steam, to start with," she said. "Chances are this wood was glued together. And we need to find some sandpaper as well."

"To sand off the finish so we can see the seams," he said, nodding. "I'll be right back, I think I know where some might be."

He headed out the door and she took the wooden box into the bathroom shower, placed it up high, balanced on a ledge more than likely designed for shampoo or soap, then turned on the shower as hot as she could and closed the shower door.

Then she went back to sorting out all the food they had brought back from the camping store. They sure had their share of beef, chicken, and eggs. By the time they ate it all, they were going to be sick of all three.

When he arrived back with a couple sheets of coarse sandpaper, she went back into the shower, turned it off, and got the box out of the steam.

"Already done the trick," she said, carrying it back to the table in the window.

It was now clear where a seam was around the face plate where they put their hands.

And the back of the box clearly had a seam as well.

Lee went at the back with sandpaper and after a moment it was clear where the back side of the box had been glued to the rest of the box.

"Nice craftsmanship," she said, studying the box. "Why do that for something that's just going to sit in the dark in a cave?"

"I always wondered why they never updated the design of these things," Lee said. "This is exactly what they looked like from the very start. Clearly they came up with something that stopped the wood from breaking down over time."

"Ever ask Duster?"

Lee shook his head. "Never came up in a conversation."

He put on some thick leather gloves, the same type he had worn when hooking up the box, then took a sharp blade to the seam in the wood around the back.

Joan just sat there and watched, marveling at his patience and steady hands.

One hour later she was about to suggest she get them some lunch when the back of the box popped free.

"Duster, you are a bastard," Lee said, laughing as he stared inside the box and shook his head.

Joan came around the table to look over Lee's shoulder.

What she saw made no sense.

Two heavily coated wires inside led from the posts to a metal plate under the slanted wood face. One wire, before hooking into the metal plate, led to what looked to be a clock device of some sort.

The clock device was connected to the timer on the top of the box.

Nothing more.

"I clearly don't understand," she said.

Lee just started laughing and shaking his head.

She waited for him to stop laughing and explain.

Finally he did. "There is no power source in here. They used the crystal to power the box. And the wood over the metal plate is to just protect the person touching it from too much shock from the crystal, but not so thick as to block the crystal's impact entirely."

"Still not understanding," she said. "How does that make this work?"

Lee pointed to the clock-like device. "That's an atomic clock, also powered by the energy from the crystal when it is hooked up."

She nodded.

"So if we walked up to a crystal in one of the caverns with a thin board and pushed the board against the crystal, more than likely we would be taken to some random point in that other timeline. Any random point."

Again she nodded, understanding what the metal plate did now.

"So the atomic clock is a measure of microwaves sent off from electrons. Set the timer at the top which sets the atomic clock, which then, when you touch the plate, sends you to that exact time in the other timeline."

"So why is this limited to only one hundred years?" she asked.

He reached into the box and pushed up on the timer on the top of the box until it popped out of the wood.

He quickly unhooked the two wires from the timer. He handed her the small, narrow timer with nothing showing on the black face. Then he took off a small device, about the size of a silver dollar from one of the wires that had been leading to the clock.

"This is another atomic clock," Lee said, holding up the small silver thing, "that I bet is programmed to only allow the timer to be set no farther back than exactly one hundred years."

It took her a moment to understand what he was saying.

He was just smiling and staring at the small circular device in his hand.

"Does this mean what I think it means?" she asked.

He nodded, smiling. "We take this off a box and we can go home."

She jumped into his lap and just kissed him and hugged him, harder than she had ever hugged anyone before.

And she loved how he hugged her back.

TWENTY-NINE

September 9th, 2628
Boise, Idaho

AT FIRST, LEE had just wanted to take the regulator off of one of the boxes and just jump home, but the more he had thought about it, the more he realized that was a very, very bad idea.

Joan was so excited, she also wanted to just jump right now.

So after they had both calmed down, with the box on the floor in pieces, they sat at the window table eating a chicken stew and talking.

"Here is what I think happened," Lee said. "I jumped out of the institute, headed for 1955 on July 8th, 2018. Somewhere over the next month or so, someone is going to notice I didn't return. More than likely Dawn up at the Monumental Summit Lodge where I go for dinners regularly. Someone, more than likely Duster, will go looking for me at my ranch and will find me not there. Someone will unhook the box in the crystal room I left through and I won't appear. That's when they will start discussion and calculations on what to do and where we ended up."

"So we can't go back before that date," Joan said.

Lee nodded. He was glad she wasn't yet talking about how to get back to her time. They would deal with that when they got back to his time first.

"I'm pretty sure Craig was a traveler," Lee said, "so we know they sent scouts to find out what happened exactly,

which from their perspective would take very little time."

"So to keep as much the same as we can, we have to let them discover you are missing," Joan said.

Lee again nodded. So far she was following fine.

"That keeps what has already happened in place. But now comes the hard part."

She smiled. "You mean jumping back through time over six hundred years isn't the hard part?"

He laughed. "No, actually, that's now going to be the easy part. We have to show ourselves after they discover I am missing, but before they try to stop me falling off the horse."

She frowned. "Why?"

"Massive timeline disruption," Lee said. "We would be there when they go back and stop me from falling and you would then suddenly be still alive, and I would be trying to return to a place I already existed."

"And that would happen through all of the timelines?" she asked.

"Through an infinite number of timelines, yes," Lee said. "No telling where you and I might end up or if we would even be together or even know each other."

She just shook her head at that, staring down at her chicken.

"I hate that idea," he said, "so we have to be very, very careful on how we return. And what exactly we do when we return."

She nodded. "What do we have to do first?"

"We have to unplug that crystal that got us to this point and go one hundred years into the future."

Her eyes grew huge? "Why would we go back to that dead and rotting place again?"

"We need to move that crystal," he said. "To a place where it won't be unplugged for any reason."

"Who would unplug it?" she asked. "Everyone is dead."

"But if we have anything to say about it, they won't be," he said, smiling.

She stared at him for a moment and then slowly smiled as his idea of not only getting them back to their normal times, but figuring out a way to rescue people started to dawn on her.

And he loved that smile more than anything.

THIRTY

September 12th, 2628
Boise, Idaho

IT HAD TAKEN them three days to come up with their plan. The early fall days in Boise had been wonderful, with warm days and cool nights that allowed them to sleep soundly with the window in the bedroom open.

Joan had actually started to get used to the complete lack of sounds around them. She didn't like it, but she was getting used to it.

And she was loving the old Victorian mansion part of the institute, much more than she did the caverns under it.

On the first night after the discovery that they could go home, she had asked Lee what he thought had caused the deaths.

"No clue," he said. "But it didn't kill bacteria either because we have seen things being broken apart by time. Bacteria does that. So more than likely what hit this planet was something that disrupted brain functions of all living insects and animal and fish life. You're the doc, you tell me what would do that?"

She actually had no idea. But she honestly had no doubt that her focus on comas was going to now switch to a focus on what caused this massive disaster and how to stop it.

On the morning of the second day they started what Lee called, "The Great Search."

"We're looking for a very, very secret place," Lee said. "It will be a cavern with crystals. But only a few of them?"

"Why only a few?" she said.

"The founders of the institute, meaning Bonnie and Duster and Dawn and Madison and some others, are all set in timelines more than likely right before the destruction here."

She nodded, not really understanding a word he was saying.

"When you are back in a time, the wires remain linked to the crystal for two minutes and fifteen seconds," he said.

"I think I understand that at least at a surface level," she said.

"So the founders needed to move from 1880 to 2600 quickly, one hundred years at a time. Director Parks, in my time, ran all the hundreds of years of the institute. He could spend thirty years in one timeline and only be gone from the others for two minutes."

"Now that just hurts my mind," she said.

Lee nodded and went on. "So Duster and Director Parks would have to have built a special room for just their use, to make sure the crystals they were hooked up to were never bothered in any way, because the machine and the crystal exist in both timelines and everywhere between."

"So if we jump back six hundred years, the box we use will exist somewhere in these caverns for six hundred years?"

"Exactly," Lee said, nodding. "We don't want anyone messing with it."

"And we need to find that special room," Joan said.

"If we can find the room, then we can install a crystal we are going to be using for the jump from a hundred years in the future to this time, and then a second crystal we are going to be using for the longer jump to our normal time."

"And tell the founders what we have done when we get there," Joan said.

Lee just nodded.

They had no luck at all on the first day of searching. Over a dinner of freeze-dried steak and apples, which were amazingly good, Joan asked, "Which parts of this complex were built first?"

"I honestly don't know for sure on that," Lee said. "But I do know the cavern I used is the one that has been there for sure from the start. But my understanding is that all of this was built at the same time in 1880."

"I think we should search that first cavern," she said.

So the next morning, they did just that. And it was Lee who noticed some faint footprints in the dust leading from a wall at the very end of the empty first crystal room.

"Someone has been here after the disaster," he said, pointing to the floor."

Joan nodded and they went to searching.

It took them both an hour to find the hidden switch in the rock surface that opened up the cavern beyond.

It was another huge cavern and the lights came up as the door swung open. Massive racks of clothing and tables covered with equipment filled parts of the room.

The cavern was divided clearly into seven areas. Each area had a couple's name over it. And then each area was divided down again into one hundred year gaps.

The earlier years had no clothing or equipment in them, but the years labeled 2400 and 2500 were full for each area.

"There are fourteen founders," Lee said. "Seven couples. They are the only ones permitted to jump farther than a hundred years without permission from the founders. I imagine they are all set in the 2500 period."

Around the cavern were a dozen small tunnels. All had been carved to hold crystals. Lee and Joan looked into each tunnel.

Seven of the tunnels were full of crystals and glowed with the light. Boxes lined up down the middle of the narrow cavern on tables. But none of the wires were hooked to any crystal or box.

"Why aren't they hooked up?" Joan asked.

"Time hasn't got here yet," Lee said.

She had no idea what that meant.

Lee clearly must have seen her confusion.

"They put all these crystals and boxes into place back when each founding couple joined the institute," Lee said. "So they will always just go down through time."

She nodded.

"Then, as a hundred years went by, someone from the future would go back and get them all."

"Jump with them like you jumped with me?" Joan asked.

Lee nodded and went on. "They would then hook up a crystal in this cavern and jump back a hundred years, being established in the future where only two minutes was passing."

"Okay," Joan said, still not completely understanding.

"That would have been repeated onward going forward until suddenly everyone in the institute died."

"No one to jump back and bring them forward," she said.

"More than likely someone jumped in here after the disaster, saw what happened, and went back and got everyone to safety back in time."

"Thus no bodies," she said.

"That would depend," Lee said, "on if we are in a timeline that the people were saved or one that they had to die before the institute founders discovered the disaster."

"Yup, another headache coming on," she said, laughing. She was just amazed she understood as much as she did.

Now Available
**from all your favorite booksellers
in trade paper and electronic editions.**

Finally, on the third day, they had their plan in place, including ways of contacting each other if they ended up in different timelines. They told each other personal stories that no one else knew as a form of greeting.

Of course, as Lee reminded her, when they died, they would end up back in this timeline with only two minutes passing here. But neither of them wanted to be apart for a lifetime after only being together for a few days. She figured that would be awkward, at best.

"You know," she had said on the third night together in bed, "If the chance of us being separated is too high, we could stay right here. It's certainly quiet enough for us to do our work."

He had laughed. "I think we're going to make it just fine."

He had kissed her and she had felt a little better.

Then he had said, "Besides, we need to lead six hundred years of advancement and brain trusts to save this planet. And we are the only ones that can jump so far into the future."

And with that, she had known the risk was worth it. But she wanted no part of not being with Lee.

Finally, on the morning of the third day, after they had had a good, solid breakfast of eggs and waffles, they went back down to the cavern and the narrow cave with all the crystals in it.

They stood beside the crystal with the wires hooked up to a box. It looked so simple, and so dangerous at the same time.

He handed her one of the wooden boxes, the one he had taken the regulator off of so they could jump as far as they needed back in time. He had taken one apart carefully and then put it back together just as carefully so it would not be noticed.

"You ready?" he asked.

She nodded.

With a thick leather glove on, he reached over and unhooked the wire.

She found herself standing touching the wooden box exactly as she had done when they used the box the first time.

He unhooked the other wire.

"What went wrong?" she asked.

"Nothing," he said. "We are in 2728, a hundred years into the future from where we had been."

A hundred years deeper into the disaster. Not a place she wanted to be. Ever.

THIRTY-ONE

September 12th, 2728
Boise, Idaho

LEE HATED THAT they were so far into the disaster again. Hated it more than he wanted to say. But now they had to get ready to make the jump home and that was going to be amazingly hard.

But they had planned every detail carefully.

First they took the long hike back up the two flights of stairs and into the large main living room cavern, then down into the old section that he used to jump back to 1890.

The lights flickered as they went, but enough stayed on for them to find their way. Lee carried the box he had altered and Joan carried a box they had taken from the very back of the 2500 crystal room. And they carried one set of wires.

They went to the most distant empty crystal room off the hidden supply room and then went clear to the back of the very long and narrow room. They put the one box that would take them forward one hundred years on the table and then in front of it the box that would jump them all the way to their original time. He was going to need to carry that box a hundred years back into the past when they jumped.

His fear was that someone would notice these in this room that wasn't supposed to have any crystals in it before he and Joan announced their presence with Duster and Bonnie. Once they told Duster, then he could tell the others about it and the crystals and machines would not be bothered.

After getting the boxes in the room, they headed back up to the living room area and back down to the rooms full of crystals off the 2500 supply area.

As they went through all the tables of supplies, Joan said, "I sure wish I knew what some of this stuff was used for."

Lee glanced around at the equipment on the tables. No doubt for someone around 2500 all this looked normal, but he had no idea either. It would be like someone from the 1600s looking at a cell phone.

What he found amazing was that so much had stayed mostly the same. Clothing had fashion looks, but it was still mostly the same and some of the stores they had gone into seemed amazingly similar to stores from four hundred years earlier.

And then other stores in that big mall they had seen had products in it neither one of them could venture a guess as to what the products did.

They took a large synthetic fiber bag and a bunch of synthetic fabric with them into the most distant of the long crystal rooms. They also both had on very heavy gloves and they had also put on large and heavy coats. It was this part of the task that worried Lee the most.

The reason they went to the last crystal room from the door was that rooms in that position were seldom used. Everyone seemed to stay closer to the first rooms and since there were thousands of crystals in every room, that didn't make much difference.

They went clear to the back and as Joan laid out the pack on the table and put the heavy fabric in it, Lee went into the wire cage wearing thick gloves and moved toward one of the crystals in the last row near the ground.

He also had two wooden boards he had salvaged from the mansion.

He didn't want to just touch the crystal through thick gloves. He wasn't sure that wouldn't send him into the timeline. He knew that the crystals were changed out all the time over the centuries, but he had no idea how it was done. And since they were over a hundred years past the disaster, they didn't have much to work with.

But he had a hunch the crystals had an area under them that had attached to the cavern walls originally and that area would be what he would touch.

He glanced back at Joan. "Ready?"

She nodded and said nothing.

He took one of the boards and eased it into the space and tried to push it under the crystal.

The board actually pushed the crystal back and then tipped it away from them.

He had been right, the bottom of the crystal was a dark stone about three inches thick.

He made sure the bottom was showing and then picked up the crystal from the bottom.

It felt like nothing more than a rock about the size of a baseball. Not light but not heavy either. He wasn't sure what he had expected, actually.

Holding it on the bottom with both hands and keeping it away from his body, he moved back through the gate.

Joan was standing back, her eyes wide, clearly as tense as he felt.

He placed the crystal gently in the thick cloth. He turned the bottom of the crystal so it was to the side they would be carrying it and then carefully wrapped the cloth around it and then pulled the bag up around it and closed it.

Then, keeping the bag away from his body, he picked it up, making sure to stay on the bottom side of the crystal and set the bag down on the dirt floor.

Then he stepped back, sweating, even though the cavern had felt cold when they entered.

"You all right?" Joan asked.

"One down," he said. "You ready to get this into place and jump back in time a hundred years?"

She nodded and started toward the front of the cavern.

Keeping the bag as far away from his body as he could, they made the long climb up the stairs, across the large living room area, and then back down two flights of stairs to the older area. It felt more like he was carrying a ticking time bomb than a rock.

Ten minutes later he had the crystal in the lowest spot clear to the back of the long empty chamber coming off the founders cavern.

Two minutes later he had the wires hooked to the crystal and the timer set for one hundred years.

He then hooked both wires to the box and stepped back, taking off the leather gloves and putting them on the table. He picked up the box he had altered and tucked it under his arm.

"Here we go," he said. "Remember to touch the box at the same moment I do."

She nodded.

He counted it down and they touched the box.

They both then stepped back.

He put the box down on the table.

She stood, staring at the box hooked up to the crystal. "So from now on out, everything we do, we are only living two minutes in that time one hundred years in the future?"

"Yes," he said.

"Just amazing," she said, shaking her head.

And with that they headed to go get a crystal that would take them home.

THIRTY-TWO

September 12th, 2628
Boise, Idaho

GETTING THE SECOND crystal went as well as the first one had gone. Even though Lee did all the work, the stress was something awful watching him.

He got it into the slot in the rock wall just above the first one they had moved. Then they had stopped and taken drinks of water.

Then when he had the box hooked up to the crystal, he set the date on the timer to July 15, 2018, at midnight.

"That's about a week after I left the last time," he said. "I don't think we dare get any closer."

She nodded. They had talked about that and she understood completely. And they had also talked about her going back to her time as well. That conversation had ended with "Let me just see what happens when we get out of this."

"On the count of three," he said.

She nodded and they both touched the box at the right moment on the count.

Then they both stepped back.

"Did we make it?" she asked, looking around.

"I don't know," he said, first glancing at the wires on the two boxes and crystals that were there.

The boxes and the crystals were now in this time with them and in every year between now and the future point.

Lee turned and headed for the door of the long empty chamber.

He took two steps into the chamber and stopped.

She moved up beside him, trying to make sense of what she now saw.

The hidden founders' cavern was still the same, but now instead of clothing for 2500, there was clothing marked going back to 1880 and clothing going forward to 2118.

"We made it," he said, giving her a smile that she would not soon forget.

She hugged him and kissed him.

She was still over thirty years ahead of her own time, thirty years from getting to talk with Steph again, but now they had people to help them

The world wasn't dead around them.

And she couldn't believe how wonderful that felt.

There were bathrooms off the hidden founders' cavern, so they went there to wash up.

Then they went to the closed door that led back out into the large supply chamber.

There was a scope Lee had found to make sure that when the secret door was opened, no one was in the other cavern. He looked through it now.

"It's clear," he said.

They quickly got out of the founders' chamber, letting the door close behind them.

Joan was shocked at how many supplies there were in this room, ranging from clothing from 1880s to her era in the 1980s, to all sorts of guns and saddlebags and anything a person would need to go back from 2018 into the past one hundred plus years.

And at least in this cavern, she recognized almost everything.

Lee led the way into the second long chamber of crystals off the supply area.

He went down about halfway. "That's the crystal I went back into 1955."

"So they haven't noticed you are missing yet?" Joan said, seeing that the wires were still hooked up to it.

"Not yet," Lee said. "They would unhook that to try to bring me here if they noticed."

Lee led her back into the supply area and over to a spot on the cavern wall. He tapped a spot and the wall slid open showing a room behind it full of all sorts of money and gold bars and what looked to be sacks of gold nuggets.

He moved to one spot and took a few piles of bills.

"Won't they notice the money is missing?" she asked.

He shook his head. "Everyone traveling back in time is always adding to this or taking what we need. Everyone traveling in time is rich beyond our imaginations."

She nodded. She would ask about that later. She took the two stacks of bills he handed her.

Then they went out into the supply area and found him his wallet and a driver's license he had left there and then they found her a small pocketbook. They went to another area and he took her picture and created an Idaho driver's license for her as well under an assumed name from a list of a hundred.

She was just stunned by it all.

"You think of everything here," she said.

"You get enough practice," Lee said. "Some of the founders have lived for a hundred thousand years and don't look any older than I do."

She opened her mouth, then shut it. Nothing about that made any sense to her at a deep level, even though he had explained it a few times.

He then printed off two credit cards for her. "That fake name has those two accounts attached, so you can get us a hotel room for tonight. I don't dare use any of my accounts."

"How are we going to get out of here?" she asked, looking at the name Joan Stevens on the cards before tucking them into her small purse with the cash he had given her.

"Follow me," he said.

She followed him out of the cavern and then up just one flight of stairs to a door they had passed a number of times in the future.

He opened it and the lights came up in a long tunnel.

They didn't talk as they went down the long tunnel that must have gone under the living room area cavern.

The tunnel ended at a staircase and she followed him up those and to another tunnel which eventually opened into a large garage.

There had to be twenty or more large cars in the garage, all white, all with a

Cadillac symbol on them, but they sure didn't look like any Cadillac from her time.

There were a couple spots empty in the garage.

Lee picked one of the cars about five deep and climbed in while she climbed into the passenger side.

"Wow, this is something," she said, looking around at the large interior and the leather seats and some sort of small screen that came up out of the dashboard.

"Duster believes that anyone in the institute needs to ride in style," Lee said. "These are mostly for the researchers who don't travel in time and know nothing about the area under the institute."

"How many actually know about the institute caverns and traveling in time?" she asked as he got the car out and along the driveway and up onto Warm Springs Ave.

"At this moment in history," he said, "Only about thirty people, counting you and me."

She just shook her head and watched the night lights go past. How in the world had she gotten into this? Someday, when things slowed down, she would have to figure that out.

Now, though, as they drove along, she at least recognized everything. Thirty years since her time had changed things, but not that much on the surface.

"I sure love that there are people around us," Lee said, shaking his head. "Can't believe I actually said that."

"I'm just glad I'm here with you," she said.

He smiled at her. "I feel the same way. And I think after all this, I owe you a late dinner, don't you?"

"Not camping food, I hope," she said.

He laughed. "Not a chance."

They had a wonderful late dinner at Denny's and then they checked into a suite at a hotel near the freeway where in her time there had only been sagebrush.

But the suite had a hot tub and she wasn't sure which one of them enjoyed it more.

THIRTY-THREE

July 16th, 2018
Central, Idaho

THEY HAD DECIDED that the best way for them to actually watch when Duster and the rest discovered he was missing was in Lee's ranch. He had told her about his secret rooms behind his home and that Duster would know better than to try to open the rooms.

So after a nice breakfast in a restaurant near the hotel, they climbed back into the large white Cadillac and headed north out of Boise.

The only difference Joan said she noticed now was that there were a lot more houses out in this direction than in her time and the road was wider.

For Lee, the drive felt comfortable. He always made this drive alone, but now, with Joan sitting beside him, he enjoyed it even more.

About two hours later they stopped in a small restaurant in Cascade and had lunch, then they bought enough grocery supplies to last them for a month or more and a couple of backpacks to carry it all. They were going to have to leave the car down near the main road because he didn't want to take any chance Duster would see it up by the ranch house.

Lee figured that it was critical to all the timelines that everything unfold without major decision points.

They went through just below the small town of Yellow Pine and then turned up the road toward the two old mining towns of Big Creek and Edwardsburg.

The gravel road was one car wide and wound back and forth. The big Cadillac SUV took most of the bumps out of the drive and made them comfortable, even though the morning was heating up. But Lee could tell that Joan was feeling a little uncomfortable with the road.

"Never been up this way before?" he asked.

"On this adventure, I'm seeing parts of my home state I never knew existed."

"Back in 1890 when I first built the ranch, this was not much more than a horse trail," he said.

She looked at him for a quick second, then went back to keeping her eyes on the road. "How did you build something up here?"

"Cut one log, one board at a time," Lee said.

Again she just glanced at him and then shook her head and went back to watching the road.

As he reached his road, he pulled off and stopped.

"That's my road into my ranch," he said.

A large pine tree was down across the road, blocking it completely. He had a chainsaw up in the barn, but he didn't dare clear the tree until after Duster showed up to try to find him.

"So what are we going to do?" she asked.

"Let's unload the stuff here and then go hide this car," Lee said. "This is going to help us be more comfortable."

"The tree?" Joan asked.

"The tree," Lee said. "Duster is going to have to walk in as well. See that small wooden plank nailed to that tree about twenty feet in the air?"

Some Classic Dean Wesley Smith Stories
Available at your favorite booksellers.

He pointed up into a nearby tree.

"The old weathered board?" she asked.

Lee nodded. "That's hiding a camera so we can see and hear when Duster gets here and starts to walk up. I also have motion sensors along the road up to my place."

"Never liked to be surprised, huh?" she said.

"I lived here from 1890 onward," he said, smiling at her as he climbed out into the heat of the high mountain air. "Never knew who was coming up this road."

He stood and took a deep breath of the hot pine scent. It was wonderful to be home.

He just hoped Joan would love his ranch as much as he did. For the first time in all the hundreds of years since he built it the first time, he was actually excited to show it to someone.

THIRTY-FOUR

July 16th, 2018
Central, Idaho

JOAN WAS STUNNED at the beauty of the high mountain valley and the heat of the midday sun as it hit her.

They quickly unloaded their supplies from the back and put them off to one side of the road in the shade near the start of Lee's road, on the other side of the downed pine tree.

Lee had made sure that no car from the road could see the supplies.

Then they climbed back into the large Cadillac and kept going a short distance up the road.

Lee pulled the car off the main road and went up what looked to be no more than a trail.

After about a hundred yards, he turned the car around in a wide area and pulled it off into some brush, headed downhill.

"No one can see the car from the road here," he said, climbing back into the heat.

They walked at a very slow pace back up the road to where they had left the groceries and supplies. Joan could already feel the heat beating at her and she was short of breath.

He dug into one of the coolers they had packed with ice and gave her a bottle of ice water and took another for himself. Then he indicated she should sit on the cooler.

"If you hear a car coming from either direction along the road, hide back there in the brush and stay low until it passes."

She nodded. "Why are you going in alone?"

"I have a four-wheeler in my barn that we can haul all this stuff up the hill with. You are not used to this altitude or heat, so no point in you walking it."

She had never seen a four-wheeler, but she was grateful that she didn't have to walk. She wasn't sure in this heat and high mountain altitude, if she would have made it very far. But she had been willing to try.

"Are you going to be all right?" she asked. "Your feet still aren't healed."

"I'm going to be fine," he said, coming over and kissing her. "Just stay in the shade and drink water. It will take me about twenty minutes."

"Be careful," she said.

With that, he turned and headed up the road, carrying the bottle of water.

She watched him walk, marveling at how handsome he was from behind, until she couldn't see or hear him anymore.

She really, really was falling in love with him. And was always surprised at how smart he was and how he thought every detail through.

Then she turned and looked around and down the road. The silence again surprised her.

Only the warm wind through the high pine trees broke the silence.

And then she heard the buzzing of a mosquito and it actually made her smile.

The silence wasn't because everything had died.

The silence was because she was in a beautiful place high in the mountains, waiting for a man of her dreams to come and pick her up.

She was still a long ways from her home in Boise and over thirty years in the future, but she had no doubt they would deal with that problem later, if there was a solution to it.

And right now, sitting here in these beautiful mountains, she wasn't sure if she wanted to go home again. She knew that she and Lee had an entire world to save, if that was going to be possible.

But, of course, from what Lee had said, their future now depended on how well this next part of his plan went. When they tried to talk about what would happen if they were too late and Duster and Bonnie had already sent people back to stop him from falling off that horse, Lee had just gone white and shook his head.

"The mess in the timelines around us would be too much to imagine," he had said. "I have no idea where we would end up."

That statement had scared her more than she wanted to think about. Suddenly finding herself in those crystal caverns once had been enough.

And the last thing she wanted to do was go back to that dead world.

Or be anywhere without Lee at her side.

THIRTY-FIVE

July 16th, 2018
Central, Idaho

IT HAD TAKEN Lee just over thirty minutes to walk up to the ranch, get the keys to the four-wheeler and get back down the road. He couldn't believe how great it felt to be home again.

And how nervous he felt about showing his ranch to Joan.

The four-wheeler had a bed in it that could carry all their supplies and Joan climbed on behind him on the driver's seat and hugged him as they started slowly up the road.

When the cleared the trees into the meadow below his ranch, he heard her gasp.

"Is this yours?" she said. "It's beautiful."

He looked ahead, trying to see it through her eyes. The tall rocky peaks behind the ranch house, the wild meadow, the tall pine trees shading the house. He was so used to it that it took her statement to get him to look again.

And she was right, it was beautiful.

He pulled up in front of the porch and shut off the vehicle, letting the silence of the mountains come back in around them.

"Let me give you a tour before we unload everything."

"I would love that," she said, climbing off and just staring around at the view behind them looking out over the mountains.

The sun was directly overhead and everything seemed to be in sharp relief.

Together they turned and he opened his front door for her.

"Oh, wow," she said, stepping inside.

It was still cool inside and he closed the door behind them to keep some of the heat out. He had air-conditioning in the apartment in the back, but not here in the main house. Here the cooler air of the night was what kept the house cool.

She moved around the big room, touching his table, looking at his kitchen, then moving over and touching the quilts he had folded on the back of the chair and couch.

"These are beautiful," she said.

"Thank you," he said.

She glanced back at him. "You made them?"

He nodded, realizing at that moment how proud of that fact he was.

She just stared at them, touching them gently like she might touch a pet.

"This way are bedrooms and bathroom," he said.

Nothing had been touched since he left it. He was glad about that.

He went out the back after she looked at the bedrooms and the old-fashioned bathroom with the claw tub and all.

They walked under a covered walkway to what he called his barn.

"Horses off to that side," he said, noting the stalls. "The other side is for tools and such I don't need to hide."

She nodded.

He went to the back stall.

"Pay close attention to this," he said. "You are the only person in the world who knows how to get in here besides me."

She seemed surprised by that, but she watched him carefully.

He pulled down on a nail on a beam, then pulled on a board on the other side of the stall.

He heard the click loudly as it echoed in the empty barn.

"Got to do them in that order," he said.

She nodded.

An old metal box had appeared near the front of the stall when he pulled on the board.

"I have now disarmed the explosives that guard this place," he said.

"Why explosives?" she asked, looking around, worried.

"I take a lot of modern equipment and supplies into the past to work on," he said. "I promised Duster and the institute that the future equipment would never be discovered if something happened to me in any timeline."

She nodded, clearly understanding.

"Remember my birthday?" he asked her, smiling.

"Now that's a date I will never forget," she said, turning and kissing him.

He opened a lid on the old metal box to expose a keyboard. He punched in the numbers zero, five, zero, three, eight, six as she watched.

A hidden door in the back of the barn opened with a click.

"I normally leave that door open unless I leave or know I am going to have company," he said, then led the way through the door.

On the other side was another regular door and beyond that was his large living room area. The environmental system was holding the temperature at a comfortable seventy-two, which felt cool compared to the rest of the place and the barn.

He had fairly modern couches and chairs and numbers of screens around the room, including a big screen television on one wall.

A large kitchen was off to one side, completely modern. In every era he updated the kitchen while leaving the kitchen in the main ranch house with more of a historical feel.

"This is my office," he said, moving to a room off the main room.

Computers and screens filled three walls with his one large office chair in the middle.

He moved to the other side of the short hallway and said, "This is my bedroom and there is a modern, for this time, bathroom, shower, and hot tub back in there."

He watched as she wandered past his king bed and looked into the bathroom. When she turned, her eyes were wide.

"This place is wonderful, Lee," she said.

"You really like it?" he asked.

"I more than like it," she said, coming to him. "I love it."

She kissed him and he kissed her back and if it hadn't been for their groceries sitting in the hot sun out front, they might not have left that bedroom for a while.

THIRTY-SIX

August 7th, 2018
Central, Idaho

JOAN COULDN'T BELIEVE how comfortable it was to live in Lee's ranch. And how much she had fallen in love with the place and the man who built it.

Three weeks had passed since they got here and staying here had felt like

a vacation from everything. She knew it was going to end, but at the moment, since they had no choice, she was enjoying the time.

They had quickly gotten into a routine every day. They got up before sunrise and showered and had breakfast.

Then they went out onto the front porch to sit and watch the sun come up over the mountains.

Every morning the sight took her breath away. And every morning it was different.

He had built his ranch in one of the most stunningly beautiful places on the planet, of that she was sure.

And he told her one evening that he was starting to understand that again looking at his home through her eyes and listening to her comments.

She liked that.

Lee had figured that Duster, once someone noticed Lee missing, would stay at the Monumental Summit Lodge for the night before coming here to check on Lee.

Lee said it would take Duster about two hours after he had breakfast to get here.

So after sunrise, they went back into the modern home in the hill and closed the door. She watched news from around the world, mostly, trying to get caught up on what had happened in the world since 1986.

The thing that stunned her the most was 9/11. And then how the world changed after that.

By three in the afternoon Lee was convinced that Duster wasn't showing, so they opened the door back up and spent time both in the back apartment and in the ranch house.

But they did no cooking out there in the ranch house at all since smells from any dinner would linger and give their presence away.

Joan was completely used to the routine and was enjoying it more and more every day when a dinging sounded through the apartment. She turned off the television she had been watching. It was about eleven-thirty in the morning.

"Here we go," Lee said from his office.

She could tell how nervous he was from just his voice. They both knew that if his friend Duster made the wrong decision, there was no telling what would happen to them.

She went into his office, pulled up a chair beside Lee, and looked at the screen Lee was studying.

A man was standing outside a white Cadillac down on the main road.

The man looked to be about thirty-five and was tall with short hair. He was dressed in jeans, a dress shirt, and cowboy boots.

"That's Duster," Lee said.

They watched as Duster took out a phone.

"That's a satellite phone," Lee said. "Signals bounce off a satellite in orbit."

She didn't even want to ask how that was possible. She was coming to the point of just taking modern advancements in stride but some of them just flat puzzled her.

They listened as Duster told someone on the phone to go check on the crystal.

Then Duster climbed into the large white Cadillac and sat staring down the road.

"He's waiting, isn't he?" Joan had asked.

"He knows what has happened," Lee said, "but he will be unwilling to admit it without proof."

"You think he knows about me yet?" Joan asked.

"No," Lee said, shaking his head. "At this point he would just think I was lost in the caverns, not both of us."

They saw Duster answer the phone after about ten minutes. Then he climbed out of the car and put on a long oilcloth coat and cowboy hat. He put a bottle of water in each pocket and the phone in another and started up the road.

Lee watched until Duster was out of sight, then sighed and sat back.

"You all right?" Joan asked, taking his hand.

"Scared to death," Lee said. "Scared to death."

"You trust your friend," Joan said. "Right?"

"And he knows as much, if not more about timelines as you do, right?"

"More," Lee said. "He and Bonnie started all this."

USA TODAY BESTSELLING AUTHOR
DEAN WESLEY SMITH
AGAINST TIME
A SEEDERS UNIVERSE NOVEL

Now Available
from all your favorite booksellers in trade paper and electronic editions.

"So trust them to trust you to find a way," Joan said. "I did."

He looked over at her and smiled, then leaned over and kissed her.

"You do know I love you, don't you?" he asked.

She nodded. "And you know I love you as well?"

He nodded and they kissed again.

Then they went out into the living room to watch on the screens there what Duster did when he arrived.

THIRTY-SEVEN

August 7th, 2018
Central, Idaho

LEE AND JOAN watched intently on the big screen as Duster appeared out of the trees and paused to take a drink of water, then started across the open area toward the house.

Lee could feel his heart pounding. He had no idea what would happen if Duster made the wrong decision, or any decision at all. Lee knew that Duster had sent people back to find out what happened. But he didn't know when and that was the problem.

That decision point to send people back in time to find out what happened was the key point they had to get past before time would be in the right spot.

"Are you sure he won't try to come back here?" Joan asked.

"Positive," Lee said. "He knows I have it rigged to blow up and he doesn't know how to disarm it. Only you do."

She nodded at that.

"Why is Duster wearing that long coat in the heat?" Joan asked.

"He says it keeps him cooler," Lee said. "I think it might by keeping the sun off of him and allowing air to flow around as he walks. Never tried it."

Duster reached the house, looking around. Then he stepped up on the front porch and opened the front door.

Lee switched the hidden camera so they could watch Duster as he stopped and studied the room.

Then Duster saw the two glasses and bottle of bourbon Lee had left on the coffee table and smiled a sad smile.

"Did he understand what you were trying to tell him?" Joan asked.

"I don't think so," Lee said. "But I have a hunch he will after he gets out of the moment."

Duster then checked the back rooms and then went out onto the front porch, closing the door behind him solidly.

He took out the phone again and told whoever answered, more than likely Bonnie, that Lee wasn't here, that they should get someone headed back in time to find out what happened.

Lee sat back, feeling partial relief.

"What happened?" Joan asked as Duster said he would meet the person on the other end of the phone call for dinner at the lodge, then took another drink and started back into the sun and down the driveway.

"He sent Craig back," Lee said, letting the relief wash over him. "You know, the nurse who was there when we vanished. Now we have only one more step to get back completely."

Joan looked at him with worry in her eyes. "And that is telling Duster. Right? When do we do that?"

"Ever been to the Monumental Summit Lodge?" Lee asked, smiling.

She shook her head.

"How about I buy you dinner there and introduce you to Bonnie and Duster. The lodge has fantastic steaks and sautéed mushrooms to die for."

"I would love that," Joan said, smiling. "Do I have to get dressed up?"

He laughed. "I think this is a come-as-we-are dinner."

"Perfect, just perfect," she said.

And Lee could only agree with that. It was perfect, as long as he was with Joan.

PART SIX
A Homecoming

THIRTY-EIGHT

August 7th, 2018
Central, Idaho

DUSTER, BONNIE, DAWN, and Parks sat in silence in the back dining room of the Monumental Summit Lodge. None of them wanted to even suggest anything.

There was nothing any of them could suggest. Lee and Dr. Failor were on their own.

"If they do make it back," Bonnie asked, "how will they contact us?"

Duster shrugged. He had secretly hoped it would have been by now. But he knew Lee would be very careful to not set up any timeline issues if he could avoid them.

And they needed to do the same by not even considering making any decision on what to do or what not to do.

Duster twisted the iced tea glass in his hand, the brown tea reminded him of the bourbon and all the great discussions and drinks he had had with Lee at his ranch.

And then the image of the two empty glasses and the bottle of bourbon sitting on Lee's coffee table came back.

Duster sat there for a moment, then just started laughing.

He glanced at his phone to see the time. He had been back at the lodge for just under one hour.

He sat up and looked at his stunned friends. "Dawn, would you put in an order for two medium-rare steak dinners, bakers with everything on the side, and sautéed mushrooms?"

Dawn looked puzzled.

"And two glasses of iced tea."

Dawn seemed hesitant to move.

Duster laughed and shook his head. "Just trust me on this one."

Dawn stood and headed for the kitchen as Duster turned to Parks.

"Would you call the institute and get Craig and his wife up here as fast as they can get here? Make it a rush."

Parks just frowned and picked up his phone.

Beside him, Bonnie was looking puzzled. "What happened?"

Duster laughed. "Lee left me a message and it just got through my thick skull."

She looked even more puzzled.

Duster shook his head. "I'll explain in a few minutes, when Dawn gets back."

He might not have to explain. He might be able to let Lee explain it all.

Duster figured that Lee and Joan would have waited until Duster pulled away. Then they would have walked down the road to wherever Lee had hidden the car they were driving.

More than likely that meant they were just about an hour behind him.

He glanced at his phone again.

It had been almost exactly one hour.

Parks hung up the phone and said, "They will be here in forty minutes."

"Thanks," Duster said.

Some Classic Dean Wesley Smith Stories
Available at your favorite booksellers.

At that moment Dawn came back in carrying two glasses of iced tea.

"Put them right there," Duster said, pointing to two spots facing them at the end of the wooden table.

"I am assuming this means you think they are coming," Dawn said.

"Well, Craig and his wife are coming for sure," Duster said, grinning.

"You know," Bonnie said, smiling at her husband, "you can be a real jerk sometimes."

"Only sometimes?" he asked.

"No, I take that back," Bonnie said. "All the time."

At that moment the door to the back dining room opened and Lee walked in followed by Dr. Failor.

And then everyone was laughing and cheering and hugging.

One of the best hugs Duster had ever had was from his good friend Lee.

THIRTY-NINE

August 7th, 2018
Central, Idaho

THE AFTERNOON AIR was warm and they both carried bottles of water as Lee and Joan walked down the road from the ranch.

It seemed to Lee that they had done a lot of walking together over the last month and he hoped that he and Joan would continue that for a very, very long time to come.

From the moment Duster pulled away from the bottom of the road, it took them almost an hour to get down the road and around the fallen tree and then to where they had hidden their car.

Lee got it going and Joan said simply, "That feels wonderful."

The air-conditioning cooled them both off quickly and Lee had to admit, it did feel great.

For the next almost two hours, it was everything he could do to just drive at a safe speed

Joan seemed more at ease with the mountain road than she had been when they had first arrived at the ranch. It seemed she had come to really love the mountains in the last three weeks.

They made it to the massive Monumental Summit Lodge safely and Lee parked beside Duster's white Cadillac.

Then they walked over to the edge of the parking lot near the lodge. From there they could see out over the Monumental Valley and the mountains of the Idaho Primitive Area. The view must have stretched for over a hundred miles, at least.

The sun still had most of the mountains in bright light and the sky was a deep blue, but the valleys were shrouded in shadows, giving everything a sharp contrast.

"This is just stunning," she said softly, as if afraid to breathe.

Lee knew how she felt. The view often did that to him as well.

"How they knew I was missing," Lee said, "is because I come up here for dinner two or three times a week in the summer."

He pointed to the long patio facing the fantastic view that ran along the face of the lodge. Numbers of people were sitting on that patio now.

"I eat on the patio when I can."

"I don't blame you," she said, taking his hand and squeezing it.

"You ready to meet some friends?" he asked.

She laughed. "I've been ready since we ended up in that crystal cavern."

With that, hand-in-hand, they headed inside the lodge.

"Oh, wow," Joan said, looking around. "I had heard this place was spectacular, but nothing I had heard describes anything like this."

She stopped and just stared at the huge polished log beams and the turn-of-the-century furnishings. A good fifteen people were seated in the main dining room and someone Lee didn't recognize stood behind the frond desk counter.

"Ready?" he asked after a moment of letting her look around.

"You think they know we are coming?"

"I'm betting that Duster figured it out by now," Lee said. "Impossible to get something past that man for long."

She nodded, brushed back her hair, and said, "Let's go see if we have a future."

He kissed her and then led her through the dining room and to a door in the log wall in the back.

As they opened the door and stepped inside, the cheers exploded from the four people in the room.

As did the hugs and the laughing and everything else.

Then Duster pointed to where two glasses of iced tea were waiting. "Figured you two would be thirsty."

Lee glanced at Joan who just smiled and they sat down.

"So Duster's being a jerk and not telling us how you got him a hint," Bonnie said.

"We drink bourbon when he comes to talk," Lee said. "So I put out a couple glasses and a bottle of bourbon on my coffee table."

"And you both were hiding in the back?" Dawn asked.

"For three weeks," Lee said. "We got back on the 15th of July."

Parks looked at Lee. "Why couldn't you tell us then what happened?"

"Because you had already sent someone to find out what happened," Lee said. "To avoid timeline problems, we had to wait until you discovered I was missing and you sent people to find out what happened. You did that just this afternoon."

At that point Duster picked up the phone and said to someone on the other side. "Lee and Dr. Failor are here and fine."

He nodded and hung up.

Joan smiled. "Please call me Joan."

Both Duster and Bonnie nodded.

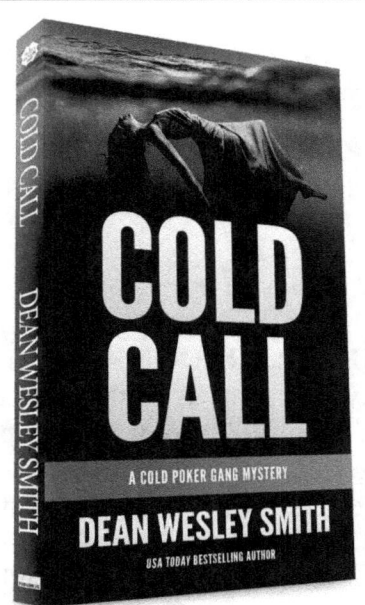

Now Available
from all your favorite booksellers
in trade paper and electronic editions.

"Talking to Brice and Dixie?" Lee asked. "How close did they pinpoint where we landed in the caverns?"

"One hundred and twenty years after the event," Duster said. "If you two walked at a good pace."

Lee glanced at Joan and then said, "Wow, they are good."

"And how are your feet?" Dawn asked.

Lee smiled. "Thanks to the doc here, I still have both of them. We wouldn't have made it out of there and through all that destruction if we hadn't worked together."

At that moment two of the most wonderful-smelling steaks arrived.

Between bites, Lee and Joan took turns telling everyone about the journey.

FORTY

August 7th, 2018
Central, Idaho

THE STEAK HAD to be the best steak Joan ever remembered eating. Ever. And wow had Lee been right about the mushrooms. They just seemed to melt in her mouth.

And the laughter and clear caring and friendship from Director Parks, Dawn, Bonnie, and Duster was amazing. They had all just instantly included her as part of their family.

And she felt very, very honored to be with such fantastic minds and wonderful people.

So when they got all done with dinner, Duster laughed. "Looks like we have

two more founders since you found our hidden area."

"I think that's only fair," Bonnie said, nodding.

"We are honored," Lee said.

Joan didn't know what to say.

"And all of us are now the only ones who know the secret of the one-hundred-year limitation," Duster said. "Can you all please keep that to yourselves?"

Both Lee and Joan laughed. "Not a word."

As they both started working on pieces of wonderful cherry pie, Bonnie looked at Joan. "I am assuming," Bonnie said, "that you are curious about what happened after you left 1986?"

"I am," Joan said.

"And you might want to go home for a time?" Bonnie asked.

Joan actually shrugged at that. She wasn't sure if she did or didn't. She knew Lee couldn't go back there, so doing so without Lee at this point didn't feel right. But she really missed Steph and she felt like her work was left unfinished.

"Well," Bonnie said, glancing at Duster, who nodded that she should go on, "Let me tell you what happened when you two vanished out of thin air. Basically, we covered it up."

"How did you do that?" Lee asked.

Joan felt completely surprised at that. She couldn't imagine how they could have explained away two people vanishing from a clinic room.

"Craig was there, one of our people, on your staff," Duster said.

Joan smiled at Lee who smiled back. "He said he thought Craig was a traveler," Joan said, "which is how he knew we couldn't just tell anyone we were back until this moment."

Bonnie nodded. "We faked Lee's death and then had you go on a long research trip. We added in extra funding to your lab and got in some new doctors and let it grow. Your clinic is now doing some cutting-edge research on the brain."

Joan didn't know what to say. She sort of shuddered, doing her best to not cry, and nodded a thank you. Lee put his arm around her, clearly understanding how important that was to her.

"Can I ask what happened to Steph? Did she ever recover from me vanishing?"

At that moment, behind them, the door to the dining room opened.

"You can ask her yourself," Bonnie said, smiling.

Lee glanced back and then said, "I'll be go to hell."

Joan turned around and there stood both Craig, the nurse, and Joan's best friend Steph.

Joan knocked over her chair to get to the wonderful hug from Steph.

And for a minute both women just cried and laughed and hugged as the rest of the room applauded and smiled.

Now Available
from all your favorite booksellers
in trade paper and electronic editions.

Her clinic was fine, Steph was here, and Lee was here. There was no reason to go back now.

This was her new home.

FORTY-ONE

August 7th, 2018
Central, Idaho

HAND-IN-HAND, LEE WALKED Joan out into the cool air on the deck overlooking the now dark Monumental Valley. The stars in the clear sky seemed to light up everything. And the air helped clear his mind.

With her at his side, he seemed to see everything differently.

Clearer.

For the past three hours they had enjoyed the company of friends. Lee couldn't believe that Joan's best friend who she had mentioned a few times was a traveler as well.

It seems that Steph had gone back to college as her cover, even though she had two doctorate degrees in areas of history in 2018. Both she and Craig hadn't been born yet in 1986, so when another scout sent back discovered that Lee would be taken to the Failor Center, Craig and Steph went back and put themselves on paths to get to the Failor Center.

Steph had never planned to become such good friends with Joan. And had been shocked when Joan disappeared with Lee.

So the fact that Joan had been taken when Lee vanished had changed their plans completely

She and Craig had decided to stay on at the clinic for another five years to make sure the center kept going with Bonnie and Duster's help. Steph said those five years not knowing what had happened and if Joan would survive were the hardest years she ever spent.

Joan felt bad about putting Steph through that.

Joan was really looking forward to finding out more about Steph's life in the morning. Her real life.

"So now what are we going to do?" Lee asked as they stood in the cold air.

Joan turned to him. "You said it yourself about six hundred years in the future."

Lee frowned. "You mean we head the effort to see what we can do to save humanity?"

"Yes," she said. "But only if we do it together."

He let go of her hand and then put his arm around her. "You actually think we can do that?"

She laughed softly. "I didn't think we could make it back here. So who knows what we can do when we set our minds to it."

He looked down at her face, lit up only by the faint lights from inside the lodge and the stars overhead. She was the most beautiful woman he had ever met and also the smartest.

He kissed her lightly, then looked back out over the darkness of the valley and the faint outlines in the starlight of the mountains beyond.

"We have six hundred years of brain power to recruit from," he said. "And that means we are going to have to learn how people just before the event lived."

"Sounds like a challenge," she said. "You think Bonnie and Duster and the institute would be up for the challenge as well, the change of focus?"

Lee nodded. "I do. Bonnie and Duster love the past, love mathematics, love people. I can't imagine how they feel about their future being cut off suddenly."

Joan nodded.

"But we would need to ask them in the morning. Think Steph and Craig would be willing to help us?"

"I'm betting they would," Joan said, smiling at him.

They stood there staring into the beautiful night air. Lee had known his life had changed the moment he realized what had happened to all of humanity.

He knew that he would never again be satisfied just going to his ranch back in history and spending the time alone studying patterns in time. That seemed so small now.

"You know," he said to Joan. "I really love the past."

"I know, she said, hugging him.

"But the past, even now, this present time, seems pointless knowing there is no future."

"So we save the future," she said.

"I like that," he said. "We do that and we bring the value back to the past."

"Exactly," she said.

They stood in silence staring out over the wilderness and all the stars.

"If you don't mind," she said, "right now I want to crawl into a nice warm bed with you and just hold you. And let you hold me."

"That idea I like a great deal," he said. "We can start all the planning tomorrow."

"Because there will be a tomorrow," she said.

"Yes," he said as they turned back into the lodge to head to their room. "Now there will be."

Coming Next Issue in *Smith's Monthly*

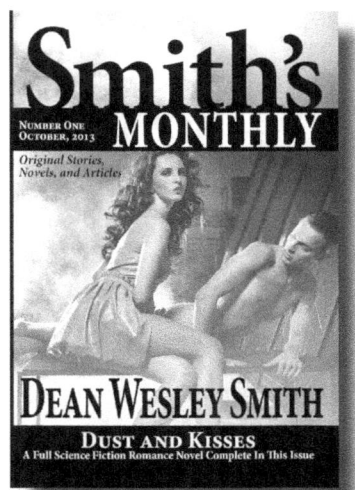

#1...October 2013

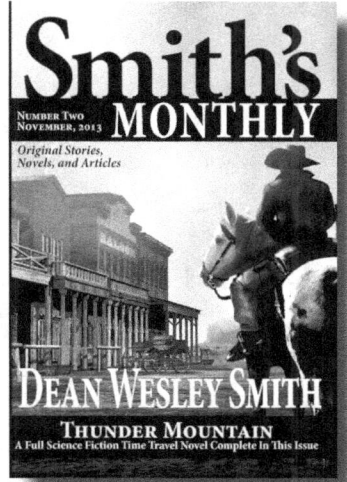

#2...November 2013

#3...December 2013

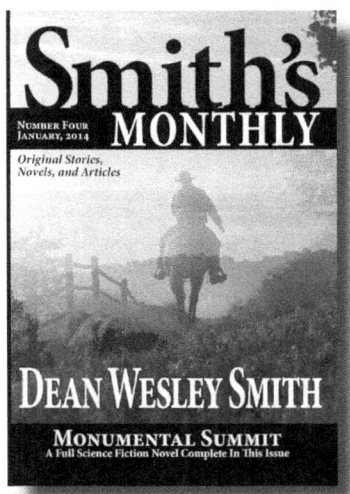

#4...January 2014

#5...February 2014

#6...March 2014

#7...April 2014

#8...May 2014

#9...June 2014

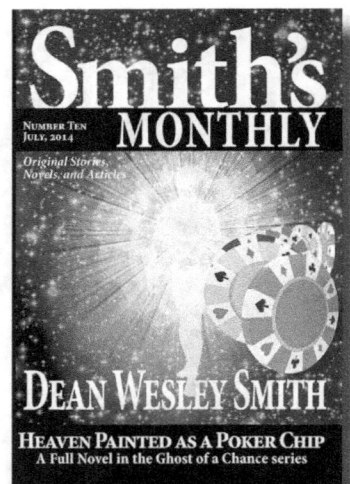

#10...July 2014

#11...August 2014

#12...September 2014

#13...October 2014

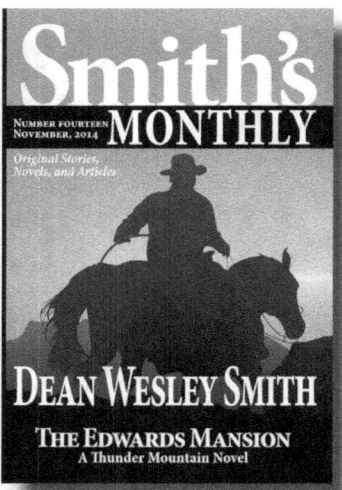

#14...November 2014

#15...December 2014

#16...January 2015

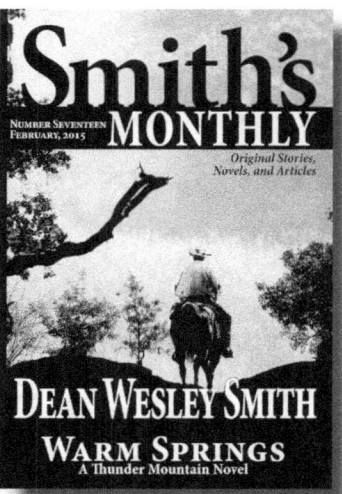

#17...February 2015

#18...March 2015

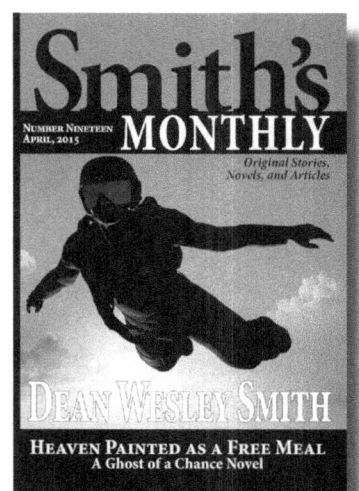

#19...April 2015

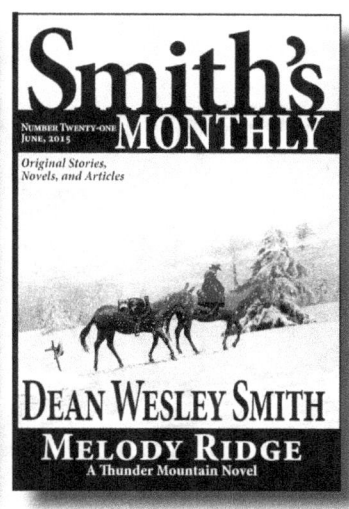

#20...May 2015

#21...June 2015

#22...July 2015

#23...August 2015

#24...September 2015

#25...October 2015

#26...November 2015

#27...December 2015

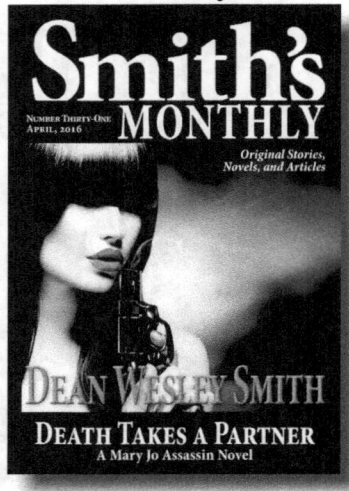

Thank You!!

I would like to thank the following wonderful people who support my blog and my work through Patreon. Your support is very important to me. Thanks!

Betsy Wilcox	Erick Lindman
Irette Y. Patterson	Christopher Ridge
Kathryn Rooney	Terry Mixon
Wendy Lee Maddox	James Husun
Jamie Curierre	Sherman Cox
Chris Cousino	Chong Go
Jane Lawson	Maria Grace
Shantnu Tiwari	Grondpom
Miguel Angel Alonso Pulido	Fen
Nancy Hendrickson	Robin Brande
Ryan M. Williams	J.R. Murdock
Jacob Proffitt	Kathleen McClure
Marian Goldeen	Gunnar Gunderson
Gary Speer	F.I. Goldhaber
Megan Bryce	Mary Jo Rabe
Michelle Tatam	John Kilgallon
Ann Tucker	Dave Hendrickson
Kari Wolfe	Jabberwocky
Albert Lemke	Eric Goebelbecker
Stacey Larson	Marsha Kessler
Diane Darcy	Scott Gordon
Krystle Jones	Martyn Folkes
Kari Gallagher	John
T. Thorn Coyle	Cj Lehi
Tasha Turner Lennhoff	Brenda Smith

www.ingramcontent.com/pod-product-compliance
Lightning Source LLC
Chambersburg PA
CBHW081153170626
46813CB00009B/3178